If Shea could just show Jared just what he'd been missing—

the warmth, spirit and traditions of a Christmas in Quiet Brook, as well as the fun—maybe she could get him to understand where she'd been coming from. He might even feel some of the things she did about close family ties and loving relationships, and then be in a better position to enjoy his child when it came.

She interlaced her fingers and gazed down at her tummy. With Jared wanting to let her go, it wouldn't be easy, but somewhere inside her, a tiny bit of hope curled right next to her baby somewhere under her heart....

Dear Reader,

Happy Holidays! Our gift to you is all the very best Romance has to offer, starting with *A Kiss, a Kid and a Mistletoe Bride* by RITA-Award winning author Lindsay Longford. In this VIRGIN BRIDES title, when a single dad returns home at Christmas, he encounters the golden girl he'd fallen for one magical night a lifetime ago. Can his kiss—and his kid—win her heart and make her a mistletoe mom?

Rising star Susan Meier continues her TEXAS FAMILY TIES miniseries with *Guess What? We're Married!* And no one is more shocked than the amnesiac bride in this sexy, surprising story! In *The Rich Gal's Rented Groom,* the next sparkling installment of Carolyn Zane's THE BRUBAKER BRIDES, a rugged ranch hand poses as Patsy Brubaker's husband at her ten-year high school reunion. But this gal voted Most Likely To Succeed won't rest till she wins her counterfeit hubby's heart! BUNDLES OF JOY meets BACHELOR GULCH in a fairy-tale romance by beloved author Sandra Steffen. When a shy beauty is about to accept *another* man's proposal, her true-blue *true* love returns to town, bearing *Burke's Christmas Surprise.*

Who wouldn't want to be *Stranded with a Tall, Dark Stranger*— especially an embittered ex-cop in need of a good woman's love? Laura Anthony's tale of transformation is perfect for the holidays! And speaking of transformations... Hayley Gardner weaves an adorable, uplifting tale of a Grinch-like hero who becomes a Santa Claus daddy when he receives *A Baby in His Stocking.*

And in the New Year, look for our fabulous new promotion FAMILY MATTERS and Romance's first-ever six-book continuity series, LOVING THE BOSS, in which office romance leads six friends down the aisle.

Happy Holidays!

Mary-Theresa Hussey
Senior Editor, Silhouette Romance

Please address questions and book requests to:
Silhouette Reader Service
U.S.: 3010 Walden Ave., P.O. Box 1325, Buffalo, NY 14269
Canadian: P.O. Box 609, Fort Erie, Ont. L2A 5X3

A BABY IN HIS STOCKING

Hayley Gardner

Silhouette
ROMANCE™
Published by Silhouette Books
America's Publisher of Contemporary Romance

To people who are there for others, like Jennifer S.,
and the whole Aut-2B-Home E-mail group.
I don't know what I would do without you!
Thank you.

 SILHOUETTE BOOKS

ISBN 0-373-19341-6

A BABY IN HIS STOCKING

Copyright © 1998 by Florence Moyer

Printed in U.S.A.

Books by Hayley Gardner

Silhouette Romance

A Baby in His Stocking #1341

Silhouette Yours Truly

Holiday Husband
The One-Week Wife
The One-Week Baby

HAYLEY GARDNER

While the teachers lectured, Hayley used to sit in high school history classes and write romances in her notebook instead of notes. That turned out just fine, because she could always study the textbooks, and the teachers always thought she was their most conscientious student who took down every word they said!

Now, years later, she is thrilled to be following her dream of full-time writing—when she isn't homeschooling her son, that is. Any free time Hayley has is spent with her husband or researching methods of teaching children with autism or collecting dolls or knitting or taking long, deep breaths…and hoping her readers enjoy her efforts to make them smile and feel good about love.

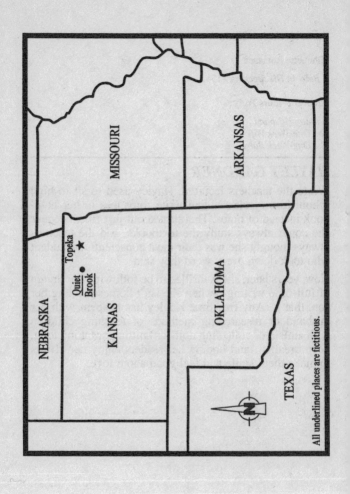

NEBRASKA

MISSOURI

Topeka
★
Quiet
Brook

KANSAS

ARKANSAS

OKLAHOMA

TEXAS

N

All underlined places are fictitious.

Chapter One

In her office at the department store owned by her family, Shea Denton Burroughs dropped the telephone receiver into its cradle and leaned back in her executive chair, the breath knocked out of her. To suspect having a baby was one thing—to have it confirmed was another.

For a few seconds, she let herself be wrapped up in the warmth of the love she was feeling for her baby-to-be. Boy or girl, it would have a life in her small hometown filled with the tranquillity, love and laughter that she'd always wanted for her children—a perfect life, just like her own.

Perfect in every way except one, she thought, tears misting her eyes. Her baby's father wouldn't want it.

"Don't be sad," a child's voice said brightly from the doorway. "It's Christmastime!"

Straightening at the sight of a sandy-haired girl about four years old, Shea hurriedly dabbed at the corners of her eyes. In Denton's department store, family was tops and kids usually had free rein, so a child loose in the office wing didn't surprise her at all. In fact, at this point, the diversion was welcome.

"I'm okay, really," Shea said, smiling warmly at the child's concern. "Who might you be?"

"Santa's helper," the girl said.

"I'm glad to meet you." Shea was. The girl's reply and the beaming smile on her heart-shaped face positively charmed Shea. "I could use some help from Santa right about now."

"I'll tell him," the child promised, nodding solemnly. "But he'll need to know your name."

"It's Shea Burroughs." Widening her smile a little, Shea added, "Could you also please let him know I've been a very good girl all year?"

The little sweetheart giggled. Still smiling, Shea bent over to get a candy cane out of her desk drawer. But when she looked up, the treat in hand, the girl was gone. Shea rose and went to check the hallway, but the tyke, one of the very few in the small town of Quiet Brook whom she did not know, was scurrying down the hall toward the escalators.

Santa's helper. Smiling at the thought of the day when her own little baby would come up with adorable answers like that one, Shea returned to her desk, sank into her chair and dropped the candy cane back into the drawer.

Frowning, she began writing a list of what the baby would need, but she wasn't really seeing the words.

She would have to tell Jared about the baby, and she wasn't looking forward to it. In a little over a week, she'd be getting a divorce from the man who had turned from the husband of her dreams into someone cool and distant she no longer knew—a change that had started when she'd made the mistake of wanting a baby too soon.

It wasn't as if she hadn't told him before they were married that she wanted children. She had. She'd also told him she dreamed of raising her babies in her own hometown, where they would have traditions and values and a grandpa—her dad—who would love them just as her granddad had loved her. Jared had just nodded and said in a couple of years they might be ready. She'd said she would wait.

But last December, when her dad admitted to having heart problems, Shea had remembered the way her own granddad had died unexpectedly right in front of her. She'd known then there was no time to waste in starting the perfect life she'd planned. So on Christmas Day she'd asked Jared for a baby.

He'd said no, he wasn't ready yet, and that had been the beginning of the end. The more she'd tried to persuade him, the more distant he'd become. Finally, he'd admitted he wasn't the paternal type and doubted that he would ever be. It was in April, when she told him she wanted to get away by herself for a while to think things over, that he'd announced he was letting her go so she could find someone else who could make her happy with the life and children she wanted so badly.

They'd remained apart until three months ago,

when, on their first wedding anniversary in late September, she'd wanted to at least try a reconciliation. Drawn by need, they'd gotten only as far as the bedroom. The morning after, when she tried to talk to him about children, he'd told her nothing had changed. He was still letting her go. She could fall in love with someone else and have the perfect, fairytale life she'd always dreamed of. So she'd filed for divorce.

He might be letting her go, she thought, but he was crazy if he thought she would ever fall in love again. She had picked the perfect man for herself the first time, dang it, and having it end between them had just hurt too much. Especially now. The love she had felt had finally given her the child she always wanted, but not the man. With a sigh, she stared down at her list and continued writing.

A slight sound at the door made her look up, expecting to see her little Santa's helper, or her father, or one of the clerks downstairs. The person she didn't expect to see was Jared.

Shea stared at him, trying to gather her wits. He lived an hour away in Topeka—so what in the world was he doing here?

Shea looked shocked, Jared thought as he stared at her wordlessly. He'd been sent up to her office with a message, but for the life of him, he couldn't find his voice. The second he'd seen her again, his throat had gone dry and tight. He was dying of thirst and she was water, only he couldn't partake anymore. He'd given up that right to let her find the happiness she yearned for.

"How have you been, Shea?" he asked. He knew her father had gone into semiretirement and allowed her to take over the management of the store she loved so much after she'd returned to Quiet Brook last April. "Still running the place?"

"For now." Shea could see that Jared was watching her every movement, but she had no idea what thoughts lay behind those dark blue eyes. She never had, she realized suddenly. From the second Jared, a former Quiet Brook cop, had stopped a thief from stealing the store's receipts and hurting her dad, she'd fallen in love with him, but she'd never really known the man.

She'd been living the fantasy she'd always dreamed of.

"What can I do for you, Jared?" she asked, wanting him gone so she could have a peaceful Christmas to recover from the hurt of their breakup.

"Your father asked me to come get you. Said there's new trouble at the Santa Station. Seems Santa is sneezing and the Grinch has probably struck again. He needs you down there."

"Oh, for goodness' sake." Shea hastened toward the doorway, expecting him to move out of her way. Perfectly in tune with her movements, he did, letting her slip through, then falling into step beside her. "You should have told me about Dad first thing," she scolded, all too aware of the riotous feelings his presence was evoking in her body now that she wasn't ten feet away from him. But she'd be a fool if she gave in to pure lust again. It wouldn't melt Jared's ice-cold heart.

"I didn't because you seemed preoccupied," Jared returned. "Just like you seem right now."

With the news of the baby, she thought. She gave him a curious glance. He had a dusky five o'clock shadow she'd never seen him wear before. It lent a sexiness to the chiseled lines of his face, a haunted cast to his eyes.

As he returned her look, she imagined she saw a flicker of vulnerability in his blue gaze. But then it was gone, and she knew it had just been a romantic notion on her part. Jared Burroughs would let himself be vulnerable at the same moment that the Grinch became Santa Claus. He had always been very much in control of his emotions, even when she had walked out on him. He could be warm, she knew that, but there seemed to be some level of feeling that he just wasn't able to reach.

"So what's all this about a Grinch?" Jared asked. "Wasn't that some Christmas legend?"

Stepping onto the escalator, Shea grabbed the black grip for balance. "Some prankster has been trying to drive off our store Santas with practical jokes."

"Why is having a Santa so important?"

Surely that was obvious, she thought. But since he'd asked, she told him. "Mack and I put some of our money into renovations this year, counting on the normally huge Christmas sales to make up the difference. But without Santa, a lot of families are driving the extra half hour to the mall for the sake of the kids and spending their money there." She stepped off the escalator. "We can't let Denton's get into serious financial trouble, Jared."

Which was an understatement. They already were. The truth was, Denton's would go under if it didn't have a total turnaround in business, and fast. And if Denton's failed, Shea would lose the job that she loved and wanted, needed to keep. She didn't want her fantasy to fade any more than it already had—for her baby's sake.

A nd for her father's, Mack's, sake, too. The store had been in the family for three generations, four if you counted her, and she didn't think her father could handle losing it—and neither could she. She needed the store just the way she needed Quiet Brook, the sleepy little town they lived in, to recover from the heartache of her failed marriage.

All too fully aware that Jared was trailing her through the maze of counters and aisle dividers filled with Christmas toys, she just barely missed being hit by a shopping cart when she rounded another holiday display. Stopping suddenly, she felt Jared bump into her from behind.

The physical contact between them left her warm and wishful, two feelings she couldn't afford to associate with Jared, and she blinked hard as she waited until the customer went by. When she looked up again, Jared was watching her with a frown on his face.

He was sticking to her like gum to the bottom of a shoe, and she didn't want him to. "My fault," she said stiffly, through a throat that had seized up tightly. "Sorry."

"Don't let my presence put you in a tizzy, Shea. I'll be gone soon enough."

"The door is straight down that aisle," she said, pointing toward it. "I have a Grinch I have to catch."

A sneeze that had to have blown down at least one wall assaulted Shea's eardrums, and hurrying once again, she took a shortcut between the branches of two six-foot Christmas trees bedecked with red ribbons and lots of tinsel. A couple of seconds later, Jared muttered behind her, "Who thought up this danged holiday anyway!"

She didn't want to turn around, but then she heard the smacking sounds of what were probably, judging from the fact that decorated trees were in the aisle, ornaments hitting the floor.

Let them be the wooden ones, she begged Jared silently, only to hear his lowly uttered, "Damn!"

That did it. Turning to survey the damage, she frowned at Jared. Broad shouldered as he was, his following her through the closely placed trees had caused several ornaments to fall. He was kneeling, trying to hook a wooden rocking horse back into place, a funny, pathetic look on his face that tugged at her heartstrings.

As he leaned down, a branch smacked against his cheek. He shoved it out of the way; it hit him again. Feeling sorry for him, she went to his side and helped put the fallen ornaments back on the tree. Clearing the way, she watched as he pushed himself free with a sigh of relief.

"It's just not your holiday, is it, Jared?" she quipped, finally letting the tiniest of smiles touch her lips.

"Nope," he said. "I'm a Fourth-of-July type myself. Lots of fireworks." Reaching up, he trailed his finger along her cheek. "If I remember right, you loved them, too."

His words and his touch were filled with double meaning, which only confused her. Drawing back, she looked at him with troubled eyes. "Fireworks are the last thing I want around here in the middle of my Christmas," she told him sadly.

His warm gaze met her eyes.

"As far as I'm concerned," she added in a manner she hoped would leave no doubt in his mind exactly where they stood, "I've sworn off the Fourth of July. No fireworks—not even a sparkler. Never, ever again."

He stared at her for a long minute. "So why am I here, I wonder?"

She made a gesture of bewilderment. "Dad has some silly last-minute idea of reuniting us?"

"He'd know better than that, wouldn't he?"

"Would he?" she asked.

The question hung in the air between them until a loud voice boomed from not too far away in the direction she was supposed to be heading.

"No, Mack, sorry," the deep voice reverberated. "I'm quitting, and no one can stop me."

"Oh, sheesh," Shea said, turning her head toward the sound. "That's our Santa. Dad's waiting for the cavalry and here I am playing around with you!" Throwing up her hands in disgust, she rushed forward down the aisle, throwing a quick smile down at the same little sandy-haired girl she'd seen earlier as she dodged around her.

"I wouldn't call what we were doing playing around," Jared corrected, keeping up. "I remember really playing around with you—and it was a lot more fun than I've been having in the past ten minutes."

With his talking like that, Shea was totally unable to concentrate on the argument Santa was having with her father.

"That's not fair, Jared," she told him as they passed the gift-wrapping section. "The minute I get ready to divorce you, you suddenly find your sense of humor again."

"Missed it, did you?"

Yeah, she had. They used to laugh a lot over little things before last Christmas. After that, well, they'd stopped laughing. The thought made her hurt all over again, and her words came out a little more tersely than she wanted them to.

"Just go away, would you?" They were approaching the double line of children and the few adults who were waiting to see Santa, but who were being treated instead to a show of Santa and her father arguing about Santa's flying the coop. "I've already spent too much time worrying about you when I should have been worrying about Dad. His chest pains are nothing to sneeze at, you know."

With a suddenness that caught her off guard, Jared's hand covered her shoulder. She stopped dead in her tracks. His hand felt warm through the wool of her green-and-tinsel-knit pullover, and she missed his touch so much. Not only his touch—everything about him. Having him there when she came home every night. His smiles over coffee in the morning. Loving him.

Gazing up into his eyes, she wished she could have her happy life back again, and for a long minute, Jared looked as if he was wishing that, too. But she knew in her heart they were fooling themselves. Without his loving and being a wonderful father to their child, without his wanting the same things as she did in life, she wouldn't be happy, and he'd been right to let her go.

"What chest pains, Shea?" he asked quietly.

Her heart twisted. Jared was never effusive about his feelings, but from the solemn way he spoke now, she could sense how fond he was of Mack—and how worried about him he was.

Two ladies with their shopping carts were quickly approaching them, so, grabbing his jacket sleeve, Shea pulled him out of their way and into a side aisle between counters piled high with foil-wrapped Christmas candies and chocolate Santas. She was in a hurry to get to her father, but she thought this was something Jared needed to know.

"Dad started having heart problems a little over a year ago, and he had a scare back in May." Since she'd already left Jared by then and had been considering filing for the divorce, she hadn't felt much like turning to Jared at the time even though she had known he would come if she called. "You two have been on a fishing trip or two since then—I'm surprised he never told you."

"We talk about fish during our fishing trips," Jared told her. "Not anything personal."

"How do men survive?" she asked, her lips parting in a wry smile.

"You have a point." Jared took a step forward. He was so close now she could smell his aftershave and feel his body heat. "Maybe we should start."

"Start what?" she asked, feeling breathless and fidgety at his nearness.

"Start talking to each other."

For one long moment, she held her breath. Then, with a sinking heart, she realized what he'd meant. "You and Mack should, you mean."

His dark brown eyebrows rose in question. "Of course. Whom did you think I meant?"

"Never mind."

"Just how serious is his condition?" he asked, the confusion on his face gradually turning back into concern.

"He's been holding his own for months, but the doctor said no more stress and that he needed to step down from management of Denton's. That's why I took over here." Her eyes softened. "I'm sorry, Jared. I thought Mack had told you, or I would never have blurted it out that way."

"I know that." He did, Jared thought. And he also knew Shea would tell him if his friend was really in a bad way. So he pushed his concern aside for the moment.

"Dad's going to be fine with me watching out for him. Don't give it another thought, okay?"

He heard the compassion in Shea's voice and could feel himself begin to melt as he stood there, looking down into her evergreen eyes. For a few seconds, as he tried to keep himself from pulling her into his arms, it felt like the two of them were the only people in the store.

In the world.

"I'd forgotten how much you could care about people," he said. And he'd forgotten how good it made him feel to have her care about him. No, maybe he hadn't. He'd just pushed it to the back of his mind, the same place he pushed everything about Shea so he'd be able to manage without her.

Jared's words sent a soothing warmth through her, a wistful reminder of the way things used to be, and Shea almost smiled back up at him. But then she remembered they were getting a divorce, and she was having the baby he would never want, and she couldn't smile anymore.

Why had her father invited the man here anyway? What could he have been thinking of? All Jared's presence was going to do was bring back these yearnings that she didn't need right now.

"I know it would be easier if I wasn't here—" Jared stopped short. He'd almost called her "hon." He wanted to call her that. But he didn't know how to make the hurt that was still between them go away, short of giving in to what Shea wanted—a family. And he knew with all his heart that his becoming a father would be a disaster. She was waiting for him to continue, so he drew a breath. "But I'm not leaving until I see your father."

"Then please wait in Dad's office for him. I'll send him up there as soon as I can."

"You're sure about that?"

"Of course. The way things have been going around here, the only direction left for anyone *is* up."

"Ain't that the truth?" Jared said in total agreement. Finally turning, he left her alone, and she dove into the crowd.

Her father, by inviting Jared here, had created yet another problem for her, Shea thought, trying to get irritated with Mack so she wouldn't break down and cry about Jared. After she worked on their current Santa to persuade him to stay on, she'd get after her father to see what was going through his mind in reference to her soon-to-be-divorced husband. And she was not looking forward to it. Her dad was almost as big a handful as Jared. No, bigger. Her dad would not retreat into silence.

As Shea threaded through the kids and their moms to reach her dad and Mr. Whitney—Santa—she smiled her best public-relations smile and glanced around. All she saw were the familiar faces of her neighbors, friends and regular customers who sat nearby in the snack section watching the "fun." Surely none of them could be playing these little practical jokes on their Santas?

The mischief had started when someone had sprinkled itching powder throughout the first Santa's suit, causing an allergic reaction that had forced the poor man into retirement. With their second recruit, it had been fake snakes and a real mouse inside the Santa sack that was supposed to hold holiday giveaways. That St. Nick had run back to the North Pole with his reindeer—at least so she assumed, because he never returned to the store. And now, with Mr. Whitney, she could only imagine the worst had happened.

Upon seeing her, her father ran his hand through his thick salt-and-pepper hair in what looked like a gesture of relief, then grinned at the man in the red velvet suit who was standing at the bottom of the Santa Station's off-ramp. "Now, Santa, here's Shea. She'll explain why you can't quit."

She frowned at Mack. "You look far too happy to see me. Don't be."

To her irritation, her dad seemed to grasp she was referring to Jared and grinned even wider, as though he was quite pleased with himself. With a glance at the crowd, he said jovially, "So my Christmas present made it to your doorstep, did it?"

"I'm returning it."

"We'll see."

"No, we won't."

"I want to see Santa!" one of the boys yelled suddenly from the line. He was immediately shushed by his mother but she was too late. A clamor went up from more restless kids.

"I'll deal with you later," Shea promised her father, pushing wayward wisps of black hair behind her ear. "Go talk to Jared. He's waiting in your office." Looking thankful for the opportunity to escape, her father turned away. Before he could scoot entirely out of sight, she caught his arm and added, "Get rid of him, Dad."

One more devilish grin, and her father was gone, leaving every muscle in her body tight with tension. With that look, Mack would probably be inviting

Jared for Christmas dinner, and she would be the turkey.

At least Mack wasn't stressed. If he was stressed, then she would have to worry.

Santa started sneezing again. Shifting her stiff shoulders, Shea began damage control and tried not to think about Jared and their pending divorce or how she really should tell him about their baby—or what, exactly, her father had in store for them. Whatever it was, Mack wouldn't have a chance to carry his plan through because Jared was one Christmas present she was never unwrapping.

Chapter Two

In the end, nothing—not talking, not cajoling, not out and out bribing—could convince Santa to stay. Dog tired, upset for the disappointed kids who had to leave without seeing Santa and unwilling to face Jared again, Shea decided to postpone the confrontation she'd planned with her father and head home to put up her feet for a while.

Definitely not wanting to think about Jared's being in the same town with her, as she drove the short distance home, Shea tried to focus on how she was going to find a new Santa. Mack had volunteered for the job, but as his daughter and the store's manager, she'd already vetoed that idea. Dealing with children all day would undoubtedly wear Mack out.

Instead, she'd given her father the job of finding another Santa, which had proven difficult the first time, what with the word out about the practical joker.

Really, she had no idea what they could do now for a Santa.

Sighing, she turned into the backyard driveway, got out and opened the garage door. Her heart sped up as she spotted Mack's truck in the second slot in the garage. He'd come home, too. If he'd brought Jared...

He hadn't. She found Mack all alone at the desk in his study, paying the bills under the glow of a lamp that had been a present from her mom a long time ago. The lampshade was yellowing, but it still had the gaily swinging fringe at the bottom, and her father refused to get rid of it. Shea had longed for a marriage like that, where the caring and the good memories never stopped. She'd almost had it—until she'd wanted more than Jared could give. Give emotionally anyway, she corrected inwardly. He had given her the baby.

"I hope your playmate has gone home," she said, setting her purse on a side table.

"You're sounding more like your mother every day," Mack said, grinning up at her.

"That's good, right?" Leaning over, she kissed him on the forehead, then lowered herself into her father's black leather easy chair. "But compliments and evading the subject will get you nowhere."

"Oh, we can get to Jared in a minute." Waving his hand in dismissal, Mack swiveled in his chair to face her. "First, the most important thing—how did it turn out with old Santa?"

She sighed deeply, which said it all.

"You think it was the Grinch again, too, huh?" Mack asked.

Nodding, she kicked off her loafers and buried her stockinged toes in the golden rug. "It had to be. We found a container of some of that gag-gift sneezing powder we sell, and the nearest I can figure out, it was sprinkled on Mr. Whitney's Santa beard. As soon as he stopped sneezing, he said it was obvious someone had a warped sense of humor at Denton's, and he wasn't spending another minute waiting around for the next joke, 'cause they weren't funny."

The corners of Mack's mouth curled slightly upward. "I always said that old geezer didn't have a sense of humor."

"Dad!" she scolded, but she was smiling, too. "Just remember, I don't want you to get stressed out over this." With faked optimism, she added, "We'll find another Santa, and we'll get that Grinch."

"Darn tootin'." Her father's grin seemed awfully smug and self-assured to Shea. "I've got it all under control."

"You do?" Her eyes narrowed as he rolled his chair back to his desk, picked up his pen and resumed writing in his check ledger. "How is that possible—for you to have found a solution already?"

Her father turned just enough to grin at her again. The twinkling in his eyes seemed magical, with an extra sparkle that came from goodness only knew where. She hadn't seen him looking this happy in weeks. But instead of being comforted, the twinkle, along with his almost Cheshire-cat look, made her feel wary.

And then she knew. She actually knew. She wasn't

her father's daughter for nothing. Her mouth fell open. "You couldn't. You wouldn't."

"Of course I would." Mack returned to his checkbook. "I'm sure Jared will help us find the Grinch."

Nerves began jumping in protest all through her body. Pushing herself out of the chair, Shea walked the length of the room and back again, shaking her head in disbelief. To have to face Jared for the next week or so as the divorce crept up on them like her own personal Ghost of Christmas Future—no thanks. She couldn't do it. She wouldn't.

"Jared won't stay here," she told her father's back in a soft tone. Jared wouldn't want to face her every day until the divorce went through, either. "Has he actually said yes?"

"Well, to be honest," Mack said, still scribbling, "I haven't asked him yet. I told him to get something to eat since I had to pay some bills first before I talked to him. He's due here shortly." Pausing, Mack glanced up at her, then gave her an amused stare. "From the way you're looking at me, you want either to change my mind or wring my neck. Have at it."

"Dad," she said, her voice serious, "this is not a joke. This is my life. You are *not* going to ask him to stay in Quiet Brook. I don't want him here."

"You might not, but the store needs him," Mack said. "He's a private detective, remember? When he finds the Grinch, all our problems will be solved."

Shea closed her eyes. Of course she remembered. Jared had quit the force when her father had found out that Jared's dream was to open his own detective agency and had lent him the money. He'd already paid back the loan shortly before Christmas last year, and that had been one of the times she'd actually seen him celebrate something. He'd been so happy.

She sighed. It was time to put her foot down where her father was concerned. "You aren't harboring some hopes that he and I will mend our differences, are you?"

"Even if it is Christmas," Mack replied, then paused to lick the flap of an envelope, "heaven forbid I should waste my time wishing for that kind of miracle."

She knew what he meant. Feeling very tired, she sank back into the easy chair.

"Really, Shea, who better to find this troublemaker and give us back our storybook Christmas than Quiet Brook's former hero?"

He was referring to the time when Jared had caught their store's thief. Even so... "Jared and storybook Christmas do not belong in the same sentence. He finds Christmas painful."

Mack frowned. "He told you that?"

"Let's just say he made it clear that he wasn't interested in Christmas trees or Christmas Eve dinners." Or traditions or life in a small town.

"Maybe if he had all the fun of a Christmas in Quiet Brook, he would be," Mack said almost gently, then rose to carry his mail out of the room.

Shea doubted that. Jared had already told her he just didn't see the purpose of going through it all because Christmas was for kids—which he never wanted to have.

But now he would have to face that, willing or not,

his child was on the way. She stared, unseeing, at the doorway. How on earth was she going to break it to him? And what would he do? Run?

"A candy cane for your thoughts," her father said, startling her. Taking the sweet, she twirled it around in her fingers but didn't tell him what she'd been thinking in return. She couldn't tell Mack about the baby until she told Jared. Because Mack would ask if she had. Boy, would he ask. If she procrastinated, her father might even think it was his personal responsibility to tell Jared himself. He was that kind of man.

She couldn't let that happen. No matter how things were between her and Jared, the news that he was going to be a father after all had to come from her, face-to-face. She supposed she would have to tell him while he was here now, however she dearly wanted to tell Mack he was going to be a grandfather as a Christmas present, and Christmas was less than two weeks away.

"So, Shea, I can count on you working with Jared to find the Grinch?"

Working with Jared? Wasn't it bad enough the man was going to be in the same town? She gazed at her father, then down at the rug to hide her confusion. Could she be around the cool, indifferent man Jared had become for days, knowing that he didn't care enough about her to try to change for the sake of love?

It hurt too much, and she didn't want that hurt intermingling with her joy about the baby. She drew in a long breath. "I don't want him here, Dad."

"Hmm," Mack said, his weathered forehead wrinkling. "Well, sweetheart, I'm going to have to overrule you here. You might manage the store, but I still own it. If you don't cooperate with me, I'll just lay you off for the whole time Jared's here. Then you won't have to deal with him."

"So you're saying if I cooperate, I have to be around Jared, and if I don't cooperate, I lose my job?" Her mouth pursed as she was caught between amusement and just a little bit of exasperation at how easily he had boxed her in. "I hate you when you act like a boss." Only half-teasing, she added, "And like an interfering old—"

"Keep it up," Mack warned, "and I'll lay you off indefinitely."

Under her breath, she groaned. She couldn't lose this job. She was all set to give her child the perfect life she'd had growing up in Quiet Brook—except for the father part of it, she guessed. But more important than that, she couldn't let her father fire her because he would take her place. If he resumed the full workload she was now handling, he might end up like her grandfather had—clutching his chest, collapsing and dying before her eyes, and there'd been nothing she could do to help him. She couldn't let that happen.

"If you really think he can get rid of this Grinch, who am I to ruin Christmas for everyone?" She shrugged her shoulders and then gave Mack a soft smile. Since she was manager, all she really would have to do to avoid Jared was to delegate. Issue him his orders at the beginning of the day, then follow up later. With any luck, she shouldn't have to be around him more than once or twice a day until he found the Grinch.

She just hoped that was as easily done as thought. As she unwrapped the candy cane, she gave a sideways glance out the window—still no Jared—and then glanced at her father.

"You're awfully quiet suddenly," she said.

"I was just thinking," Mack started slowly. "Maybe you could use some of that Christmas spirit of yours to convince Jared to play Santa. It would give the two of you something to do while you watch for the Grinch to reappear. Who knows, it might even be good for him."

Jared playing Santa all day, seeing and relearning the joy and wonder of the holiday through the eyes of children? The idea brought a twinge of hope to Shea's heart, and she put the candy cane down beside her as she considered it.

If she could show Jared just what he'd been missing—the warmth, spirit and traditions of a Christmas in Quiet Brook as well as the fun—maybe she could get him to understand where she'd been coming from. He might even feel some of the things she did about close family ties and loving relationships, and then be in a better position to enjoy his child when it came.

Oh, she knew better than to expect he would change and want everything she did, and without that happening, she didn't think they could rekindle the love they'd once shared. But his having a merry Christmas in Quiet Brook could really only help him—and her baby—couldn't it?

She interlaced her fingers and gazed down at her tummy. With Jared wanting to let her go, it wouldn't be easy, but inside her, a tiny bit of hope curled up right next to her baby somewhere under her heart.

Once Mack's receptionist told Jared that his father-in-law was waiting for him at his home, Jared headed back down the escalator, scowling at the thought of what his friend might really be up to by dragging him around Shea. He nodded grimly at any number of people who wished him a merry Christmas until finally he didn't bother looking at anyone anymore. Christmas had ceased being important to him long ago—and right now, he had other things on his mind. Like Shea. Like letting her go for her own good.

Dodging three youngsters running amuck through the aisles, he bumped into a cardboard display of Santa. Both the decorations and the kids were grim reminders of how different he and Shea actually were, and he quickened his steps, needing to get out of the store and out of Quiet Brook. When he caught up with Mack, he wasn't standing for any more delays. Friend or no friend, he was putting his foot down.

Someone tugged on the back of his jacket. Turning, he had to drop his gaze way down to look into the blue eyes of a little girl, maybe five years old, one of the kids whom he'd seen in Denton's earlier that day. Her denim jacket looked a size too small and was much too thin for the weather outside. Her look of poverty reminded him of his past and made him even more eager to escape the store, which seemed to be bringing back too many memories for comfort ever since he'd set foot inside it.

"Yeah?" he asked, glancing around at the almost empty aisles. Didn't the kid have a mother?

"I know where Santa is."

"Yeah, okay." Jared knew that story. "The North Pole."

"Honest. I know where the real Santa is."

"Whatever you say." He began to sweat. Even with his time on the force, he'd never quite gotten used to dealing with children. But before he could walk away, she latched onto his jacket with a grip that surprised him.

"You want me to take you to Santa? Then you can tell Mrs. Burroughs where he is, and she can ask him to sit at the Santa Station, and then she'll be happy. I saw her almost cry before."

Oh, that was just what he *didn't* need to hear. He'd counted on Shea's return to Quiet Brook making her happy—something she hadn't been toward the end with him. The fact that she still wasn't content was unsettling as hell because he still cared. He still cared a whole lot, and he knew the mental picture of her crying would come back to haunt him in the lonely hours of the night—it already had once or twice.

"Can you come see Santa with me?" The little sandy-haired girl smiled up at him with cajoling eyes.

The cold insides of Jared's heart started melting. "No," he said, careful to keep his tone soft as he gently disengaged her fingers from his jacket. "I can't come with you anywhere. That wouldn't be a good idea. You should go and find your mom and not talk to strangers.''

''But it's okay to talk to you,'' she said earnestly, dropping her hand to her side. ''Santa said you were once a nice boy—you just grew up wrong.''

Raking his fingers through his thick brown hair as he stood there, Jared tried to figure out what exactly was going on. A stranger dressed up like Santa Claus talking to a little girl about him—and getting the information right? He decided he didn't want to know. He didn't want to get that involved with the child, the Santa Claus, or with Shea for that matter. What he wanted was to get out of her store where he could practically smell the ginger of her perfume every time he walked down an aisle.

''I don't want to see Santa,'' he told the child firmly. ''Run along and find your mother, okay?''

''You sure?''

''Positive.'' With a wave, he turned and started walking away.

The girl was probably just lonely, he supposed. Her friends must have run off and she had no one to play with. But still, it wasn't good that she was inviting complete strangers to take her someplace…not even in a small town that was quiet and peaceful most of the time.

Sighing, knowing he wouldn't rest that evening unless he was sure she had someone to watch over her, Jared began to scan the aisles, looking for the little girl in the thin denim jacket. But she seemed to have disappeared.

At the service desk, he told the clerk about the

child. She claimed not to have noticed any young girls by themselves. Everyone else he asked in the front and rear of the store said practically the same thing. Finally, he came to the conclusion the girl must have gone home, even though by the strange looks he'd been getting as he asked after her, he was starting to believe she didn't exist. That she was a little fairy of some sort, in a fairy-tale town.

But he didn't believe in fairy tales. Swearing under his breath, Jared headed toward the front again, passing the deserted Santa Station on his way out. Seeing it reminded him of Shea and her efforts to keep the Santa there. Apparently, she had lost. That didn't bode well. She lived for Christmas, and with the store in trouble, this wasn't looking to be a good one. He was used to that, but he knew it was going to be a disaster for Shea. He didn't want that for her. Not along with their divorce in just over a week. But he couldn't do a thing to help her. Not one damned thing.

Five minutes later, he was in his truck, driving toward Mack's, his face tight with tension. Their marriage probably could have been salvaged if he'd given in about having a baby, but he couldn't do that to a kid. He'd been an only child and his father had been a bitter, remote man. All Jared knew about fatherhood was what he'd learned from his own, and that wouldn't be nearly enough. It hadn't been for him.

From his mother's death at childbirth, Jared had been brought up on the family farm. The only love he'd ever known was from his Aunt Ruthie, who came most days to cook and clean. But when he was nine, she'd died of some illness—he couldn't remember what.

What he did recall, vividly, was clinging to her in the hospital, begging her not to leave him, that he didn't want to be left alone with his father, with no one to love him. Seconds later, his father had pulled him away with a look of fear and sadness on his face that Jared had never forgotten because he had put it there by his words. And his father had said something that he still remembered.

"I'm sorry, boy. I did the best I knew how for you."

After that, Jared had never mentioned anything about not wanting to be with his father again, and in return, his father had continued to practically ignore him. After a while, he guessed he had just stopped caring whether he had love in his life. Maybe he thought his father's remoteness was love. It was all he knew.

And all he could give a child.

He'd done all right alone, and would again. He'd put himself through college with scholarships, and by the time he was twenty had his degree and a job on the Quiet Brook police force. He'd kept mainly to himself for years, dating occasionally, but mostly living without love and emotion, until that fateful day when he'd gone into Denton's, saved Mack's payroll and his life—and met Shea.

When he married her, he'd known that she was too much the sweet princess in a fairy tale and he'd been too much an emotional pauper for them to ever make it together. But he'd wanted, for once, to feel like the prince, so he'd ignored all his inner warnings that their relationship would never last, that he couldn't give her what she needed most. He shouldn't have. He'd only hurt her. For himself, he didn't care, but the last thing he wanted to do was hurt the one woman who had loved him for a while with all her heart.

After parking his truck, he got out and walked up the steps to Mack's door, where he paused to steel himself against seeing Shea again. He was doing the right thing by letting her go, he reminded himself. Without him, she could find someone who would make her happy and give her the family and the small-town life she craved. He just had to remind himself not to feel anything when he was around her, to revert back to the loner he'd always been.

Ready, he rapped on the front door. Mack answered it and led him into the study. Shea was sitting in the window seat, framed by Christmas decorations of holly and ivy. The house smelled of cinnamon and sugar and…Shea.

He found himself staring at her again, even though he knew better. Tendrils of her long black hair waved softly around her face, framing it as her eyes met his with an evergreen warmth that always filled his body with the familiar heat of longing. He wasn't fool enough to believe that would ever change. He wanted her. He always would.

Her lips parted as she began to speak, but Mack beat her to it, his tone jovial. "Jared, thank you for coming."

"You said it was urgent," Jared reminded him, finally tearing his gaze away from Shea. "So what can I do for you, Mack?"

Seeing Jared standing there, rigid as a wooden soldier, Shea knew she had to carry through with the semblance of a plan she'd made while she waited for him to arrive. Every line of his face spelled loneliness. Jared needed to be given a chance to know the joys and pleasures of the season, to share in the Christmas spirit with others, and she was the only one who really still cared about him enough to persevere through the attempt. Since she already knew her marriage was over, she had nothing to lose by doing this, and her baby—and Jared—would have everything to gain.

"I assume Shea filled you in on what's been happening at the store?" her father said to Jared.

"With the practical jokes?" He nodded. Waiting.

"I'd like you to find out who the Grinch is," Mack explained. "We'll pay you, of course."

"You got me down here just to find a guy playing practical jokes?" Jared asked, sounding like he didn't believe it—or considered it a waste of time. Shea winced.

Mack nodded affirmatively, and Shea added, "Please?"

Jared turned to her. "How would you two suggest someone go about finding this 'Grinch' of yours?"

"We figure the troublemaker is more than likely someone in the neighborhood." She toyed with the drapes as if she hadn't a care in the world and as if she didn't really notice how steadily he'd been watching her. "Maybe even someone who doesn't like small towns and who doesn't have any Christmas spirit.''

That someone, Jared thought uncomfortably, sounded an awful lot like him.

"To get this guy," Mack said, taking over, "you could keep an eye out for someone lurking around the Santa Station and try catching him in the act. You could also ask around and try to find out if anyone is upset with my store."

"I'm not sure I understand why this is such a big problem," Jared said, all too aware that this remark wasn't going to set well with his friend. But he didn't want to stay. "Couldn't you just give out free candy or something to the kids at the Santa Station? You don't really need anyone to play Santa Claus, do you?"

Shea tried to think of an explanation she hadn't already given him, but her father sat down on the chair by his desk with an audible *whoosh* coming out of his mouth.

"Don't need a Santa?" he asked incredulously. "Heck, Jared, of course Denton's needs a Santa. Christmas in Quiet Brook wouldn't be the same..." Mack frowned at Jared. "Didn't Shea ever tell you about our gift-giving program? It's been a family tradition for years."

Jared aimed a long, unfathomable look in Shea's direction that had her tingling all over and forgetting, for the moment, about their present troubles and the fact that the two of them were currently as incompatible as dry Christmas trees and Roman candles.

"I'm sure she might have tried," he said, "but I'm

afraid I've never paid much attention to anything about Christmas.''

That cool tone in his voice was all too familiar. She'd heard it a lot right before she'd left him, Shea remembered. It made her sad and afraid at the same time. Afraid especially because she knew she couldn't help getting herself involved in trying to change him, and she was already feeling tender and wounded.

But she had to try, for Jared's own sake. "During World War II," she said, "my grandfather started a program. As each child visited Santa at the Station, the helper there recorded the child's name and wish on a list. Then Denton's would move heaven and earth, either through soliciting donations or giving the present themselves, to make sure the needy kids in town received at least one gift they craved.''

"The churches in town could do that now, couldn't they?" Jared asked.

"They could," Shea admitted. "Or the children could just mail their lists to Santa in the box in front of our store. But, Jared, the way Denton's department store plays Santa to kids is one of the things that helps make Christmas in Quiet Brook the magical holiday it is.''

And, she added silently, they had to get things back to normal at the store by capturing the Grinch and hiring a Santa. She didn't want to lose her job, the store, or anything else in her life.

She'd already lost Jared.

"So couldn't you consider helping us—for the kids' sakes?" her father asked.

From the way Jared was looking at her again, with

an unreadable something in his dark blue eyes that Shea couldn't figure out—but it wasn't emotion—she knew he wasn't going to stay and help by finding the Grinch, never mind by playing Santa. He wasn't, she knew, because *she* was there.

Just as she predicted, Jared shook his head. "If that's all you needed, Mack, old buddy, then I've got to be getting back to Topeka. There's work there calling my name."

The scene seemed eerily familiar to Shea. She had lived through it more than a few times since last December when she'd brought up the topic of having a baby and started pressing him to agree. Jared tended, to say the least, to avoid confrontation. If she didn't miss her guess, in about four seconds…

She was right. With a wave, he turned and walked out of the room. Knowing the importance, Shea rose and hurried after him, flicking on the front porch light on her way out.

"Jared, wait!"

He cleared the porch steps and kept walking.

"Please?" The frosty air swirled around her, but if she went inside long enough to get her coat, he would leave and she would miss her chance. "Please? We have to talk."

He stopped, his shoulders tensing, and she held her breath. To save Christmas for the store and the kids— and to help him and their baby, she had to find a way to persuade him to remain in town, even if every time she saw him brought back the painful memories of what could have been so perfect. He had to stay, only she didn't know if she could be near him without falling to pieces.

Very slowly, he reversed direction. The shuttered look on his face was one she knew well, and it occurred to her that he had completely lost whatever sense of humor he seemed to have had at the store— or he'd just been faking it all along.

Either way, she was going to have to help him find it—and fast.

Chapter Three

Walking up to join Shea on the porch, Jared watched her with shaded eyes.

"I wish you wouldn't go," she said softly, her green eyes tearing him apart. "Mack needs you here."

"I have to go." He did, because he was not going to spend the upcoming days until the divorce torturing himself by being in the same town as Shea. Instead, he would be back in Topeka, working his tail off until he keeled over. If he timed it right, that event would take place at midnight of the morning of the divorce, and then he would sleep through until Thursday morning. After that...well, after that he would try to get through his life by pretending that Shea had never existed. Reaching out, he brushed a wisp of her hair behind her ear. "Why didn't you tell your father there's no hope for us?"

"I did, Jared," she swore. "I even repeated it today. He just doesn't want to believe."

"Then I guess the question is, why are you out here trying to convince me to stay here and go through with his plan?"

"I have a couple of very good reasons," she told him. "One of them is that Dad doesn't need the strain of losing the store. The other..." Her voice dropped off. "It doesn't matter. What does is that your helping us is so important for the sake of the store, the kids, the town—everything. You have no idea." The cold was getting to her, and she couldn't hold back a small shiver.

Jared took off his jacket, put it over her shoulders and pulled it close around her. "We should talk inside."

"I think I prefer it out here," Shea said with a small, wry smile. "Mack would eavesdrop. If I can't convince you to stay, I don't want him telling me what I should have said to you that might have worked."

"Yeah, well, you're cold." Even as Jared said it, he realized *he* didn't seem to feel it. Never had. Maybe he, like his father, was really made of ice. "Mack should be the one out here."

"I'm all right." Clutching his jacket, wrapped in what had been the heat from his body, Shea shook her head. "Dad thinks I should handle this Grinch thing—and you."

"Gee, I wonder why," Jared said wryly, a trace of a smile on his lips.

She didn't smile back. "Probably because he thinks

we belong together—but I guess we proved him wrong, didn't we?''

"Yeah, we sure did.''

So much for lightening the mood, Jared thought. Unless he missed his guess, Shea was on the verge of tears. He'd already made her cry too many times. He wanted to go, but somehow he just couldn't say no to her again and walk away. Not when she wanted the help so much.

"Congratulations on the promotion,'' he said. "You always did enjoy the store and everything about it.''

"I think loving and being committed to Denton's is a requirement before you can bear the family name,'' she said.

"I'm surprised you ever agreed to leave Quiet Brook to come with me.''

"I loved you more than the store and the town,'' she admitted softly. "More than anything.''

"And I messed that up, didn't I?'' His jaw moved as he surveyed her deep green eyes and high cheekbones and found her usually expressive face unreadable. "Give me a reason to stay, Shea,'' he urged, his voice low. "One that I can understand.''

He was trying, Shea realized, only she'd run out of reasons for him to stay. The one she wanted—for him to stay for her—wouldn't work.

"How about this?'' she asked slowly, brainstorming. "If you stay and find the Grinch, you'd be saving Christmas for the needy in a small town in the heartland. A story like that hits the tabloids, and you'd be famous and get loads of publicity for your agency. What do you think?"

"I think that sounds pretty close to being exploitative," Jared said. "And cynical. You wouldn't want me to take unfair advantage of the public's gullibility, would you?"

"Yes?"

He shook his head, pretending sadness. "Being married to me has warped your precious small-town values a little. But I'm still unconvinced. Want to give up now so I can go?"

"Okay, Jared," she said, too calmly for his peace of mind, "I wasn't going to do this, but you've driven me to it. I'll beg. I'll even throw something in it for you. If I agree to be very, very, nice—" she blinked the thick black lashes of her eyes and closed the distance between them "—will you please stay and help me make Christmas special for the needy kids in Quiet Brook?"

The closer she got, the more Jared wanted to stay, and not just because he wanted her. It was everything about her that enticed him, including the fact that she cared enough about him to want to give him the family life he'd never had. She was the one woman who might have filled the hole in his life, he realized, but he couldn't let her—for her own sake.

He didn't want to hurt her any further, so he backed away ever so slightly. "I can't help you, Shea."

Her face fell. "Why did I possibly imagine mentioning little boys and girls in the store with no Santa in sight would faze you?" she asked, her voice sadder than he'd ever heard it.

Her mention of small kids brought the image of that little sandy-haired girl in Denton's back into his mind. Jared couldn't move, thinking about how that child had been so damned worried about Shea—and so certain of herself. It was almost as if he'd been visited by... No, he wasn't going to be sidetracked by the magic-of-Christmas bit. Stupid, fanciful thoughts would get him nowhere.

She'd struck some chord inside him. Shea knew it, could see the second his eyes changed. Taking a deep breath, she forged on. "There's something else."

He waited. The crisp air seemed to crackle with electricity between them. She crossed her fingers, both for luck and because of the little lie she was about to tell.

"Mack's condition is worse than I led you to believe." Maybe it wasn't such a lie. Her father's condition would definitely take a turn for the worse if Mack ever heard about what she'd just said to his best friend.

Jared hadn't been expecting that, and the news took his breath away. "If this is a trick, I'm not sure what I'm going to do to you," he warned. "But I guarantee that it won't be anything with Christmas spirit in it."

"I wouldn't tempt Fate lying about something like this," she said, crossing her fingers again under the cover of his jacket.

"You should have told me earlier." But Jared couldn't sustain his irritation, not when he was overridden with worry for his friend and the thought that if something happened to Mack, he would really be irretrievably alone—and so would Shea.

His throat went dry. Mack was the one person who had never wanted anything from him, no matter what, seemingly from the second they'd met. And Mack's loyalty was limitless. Even when Shea had left him, Mack had refused to take sides. He'd do anything for Mack—and Shea knew it.

Yeah, Shea knew it. He gave her a suspicious look. "Why didn't you tell me the truth about your father's health before?"

"I didn't want you to stick around before. Then Mack did his blackmailing bit, and now I need you here."

Jared wasn't at all worried about Mack doing anything to Shea that she didn't probably deserve, but he had to ask. "What did Mack threaten you with?"

She looked like she might not answer. As she hesitated, she moved her arms, and his jacket almost slipped off her shoulders. Without thinking, Jared stepped forward and drew it around her again. He could hear her breathing stop and then he backed away, cursing himself for losing his control. He shouldn't touch her. He really shouldn't touch her.

"Mack basically told me if I wasn't nice to you while you were here, he'd lay me off work until you left."

In the front porch light, Shea could see a slow grin cross Jared's face, lighting up his eyes. A true smile of honest amusement. Caught by surprise, almost mesmerized, she finally released her breath, which she seemed to have been holding forever. Then the meaning of his smile penetrated.

"Wait a minute. You think Mack's blackmailing me is *funny?*"

"Hell, yes. Ironic." His chuckle resonated from deep within. "Shea Burroughs actually needed to be threatened to show Christmas spirit? You were always so full of Christmas spirit, I used to think you could convince Scrooge to change into Santa Claus."

"You did?" she asked, tilting her head upward to look into his eyes, her face deadly serious. "Then why couldn't I so much as get you to like the Christmas holiday, let alone anything else?"

His laughter faded away, and he shook his head. "Because Scrooge once believed in Christmas, Shea. I never had a chance to. I can't start caring about something I never really knew. You didn't have a chance."

"So give yourself a chance now to get to know what I love in my life here, Jared. Please, just one chance? Stay?"

Jared's eyes drank in her long braid, which rested over the top of his leather jacket, the small Santa earrings fastened to her earlobes, and the delicate arch of her lips that were tinted Christmas Berry Red, a color she wore all year long. She was Ms. Apple Pie and a pinup girl rolled into one, and it wasn't taking much imagination to remember how she felt in his arms. He found himself badly wanting to kiss her. Just one last kiss to imprint upon his brain how good her mouth felt against his, how soft her hair was, and even how warm her sighs were as they touched each other.

Just one kiss...

"Jared." His name sounded breathy on her lips, just as it did each time they'd made love. "Please stay."

Hell. Maybe he couldn't feel the cold because his brain had frozen over, but there had been such hope in her voice, in her eyes... "Okay."

Those same evergreens lit up like Christmas trees. They flooded him with warmth, which made him want to jump in the lake up the road and become numb once more. Because as soon as anything started up with Shea again, he knew he was going to get hurt. It was inevitable. They were too different. They were just not meant to be.

"I'll stay for Mack's sake," he added. Or even for that blue-eyed little girl he'd seen in Denton's. But definitely, Jared told himself with great conviction, he was not staying because he had any thoughts of trying to reconcile with Shea. "The minute I figure out who your practical joker is and stop him, I'm out of here."

"Okay," Shea said, but with none of the self-assuredness her voice usually held. Not understanding what her uncertainty could mean, Jared frowned, but she had already turned away. "Let's go inside, shall we? I'm sure Dad wants to discuss payment."

As if he would accept any money for this. He followed her up the steps. This was going to be the worst week of his life, trying to save a holiday that he didn't care about for a town that he didn't care about—for a man he did care about, but for a woman he would swear that he wanted nothing more to do with. All that, with a divorce thrown in for good measure.

If he was smart, he would lay down some ground rules.

And he *was* smart. Stepping to Shea's side, he caught her hand under his on the doorknob. "We have one last thing to talk about before I commit myself fully by telling Mack I'll do it."

She turned around with a gentle smile on her face. "Whatever you say, Jared."

"Remember you said you'd be very nice to me if I stayed and did this?"

"Yes," she said cautiously.

"So how nice would that be?"

"I was thinking along the lines of baking you an apple pie." Her eyes blinked nervously. "Why? How nice are you thinking I should be?"

"Oh, an apple pie would probably be fine." He told himself he didn't *want* her to throw herself at him. That was fine. But still… "I was just making sure you didn't have anything else in mind."

"Oh, but I do," Shea said, knowing exactly what he was suggesting, but also exactly what she was referring to. "I definitely do."

She would have teased him a bit more, but she sensed something on the lawn on the far side of the house at the same time that Jared indicated her father's presence with the slightest movement of his eyes. She twisted enough to see her father carrying a bag of trash over to the curb.

"You two find any Christmas spirit yet?" Mack asked cheerfully as he walked back toward them.

"We're still looking, Dad," Shea called out, flashing him a brilliant smile that seemed to please him.

"But don't worry." Her mouth lifted into a smile for a second, and she said sweetly to them both, "Even if we don't find it, I can absolutely promise you and Jared one thing, no matter what."

"What's that?" Mack asked, joining them.

"Nothing is going to keep me from making this a Christmas Jared will remember for the rest of his life."

Mack and Jared shared a long look. Jared knew he should be worried. She was wearing a knowing smile on her face that he'd never seen before. Well, no sense in letting her have all the fun.

"It could even be that I might have something cooked up for you, too, Shea, something that you'll never forget."

A swift frown shadowed her face and then left, leaving in its wake pure amusement. "Oh, but it won't be close to my surprise, or nearly as interesting."

"Probably not, but maybe it will be an eye-opener when it comes to my vision of the real world."

"I think I might like to understand your world a little better, Jared," she said truthfully. It wouldn't change anything, because she wasn't going to compromise on her dreams for her life, but maybe it would help her explain to her child why its daddy was the way he was.

"Well, I can't claim to know what you two have in store for each other, but it certainly sounds like you're getting along just fine," Mack said heartily, grinning at her just the way he used to when he watched her in school pageants. Like he was proud of her. It was good to know, Shea thought, that she was doing something right. "Now, let's go inside and get some of that chili I've made for dinner. How about that?"

"Sounds great, Dad," Shea said. Although with Jared around, she didn't need chili to heat her up.

"I already ate," Jared reminded them. "But I'll be happy to come in and have some coffee."

"Of course you are," Mack said heartily. "You're staying—" he cleared his throat at Shea's wide-eyed look "—in the guest room."

Before she could voice her protest, her father's attention was diverted by someone across the street.

"Hello, Mr. Griswold!" he called to the elderly man picking up the evening paper from his driveway.

"Yeah, same to you." The man straightened. "Did you two catch the Grinch yet?"

"Not yet."

Nodding gravely at them, the Dentons' friend returned to his own business. Jared was puzzled. It was as though their neighbor also considered the practical joker a matter of extreme importance. Why didn't he himself understand why this mattered so much to everyone?

Mack opened the door. "You two coming in?"

"Just give us one more minute, Mack," Jared asked.

She didn't need another minute with Jared, Shea thought, reaching for the storm door, only to find Jared's hand suddenly on her arm. Turning, she could almost feel his warm breath hitting her face. He was

so close that she felt faint with wanting to kiss him—
just once more for old times' sake.

"I want you to know, Shea, that you can't really
expect anything out of this, okay? I'm only staying
to stop this Grinch for you and Mack—it doesn't
mean anything to me whether I do or not."

"I understand," she said softly. "I won't expect
anything, but I'm still going to believe in Christmas
miracles—even where you're concerned."

Before he could reply, she slipped through the door
and hurried toward the kitchen, seeking the warmth,
familiarity and relative emotional safety of her father's presence. But in the hallway, seeing that Jared
hadn't followed her directly inside, she took a moment to lean against the hall wall and recapture her
breath. She'd wanted to kiss him just then. He'd almost kissed her minutes before. The two of them were
playing with fire, and she would have to start being
very, very careful.

Outside, where Jared continued to stand, the breeze
picked up and the stars were losing their shimmer. Or
was that because Shea was no longer outside with
him?

He knew he should be following her in or Mack
was not going to believe that he and Shea were getting along. But he stayed outside anyway, wishing
deep down that Shea would want him just the way he
was, the way he'd always been. But he knew she had
her dreams, and they were too much in conflict with
his own. He was resigned to getting the divorce and
losing the only thing that had ever made him happy—
Shea.

If it wasn't for Mack, he would leave right now. He swore he would. But even so, doubts crept into his mind. Something was holding him there, and it wasn't his friend. He wasn't even sure it was all Shea's doing. This peculiar feeling that he was supposed to stay had started when he'd run into that little girl in Denton's, and he hadn't been able to shake it.

"Damned Christmas spirit," he muttered under his breath, opening the door and heading inside. He was letting it get to him and he knew better.

He really did.

Closing the front door behind him, he decided what he had to do. He would find that little kid and, somehow, figure out what the heck she was talking about when she claimed to know where the *real* Santa was. Then he would know for certain that some nut wasn't filling her head with stories for some nefarious reason and that she was safe. After that, he'd put a stop to this practical joker, get out of Quiet Brook and return to his plan of work and exhaustion, which would have to suffice.

No matter how much more he might want out of life.

Chapter Four

Shea's heart started pitter-pattering like crazy as she searched the store for Jared early the next afternoon. During a long, restless night caused by knowing Jared was only a few yards away, she had come up with the first step in a concrete plan of action to turn Jared into a Santa Claus dad. Juggling it along with the demands of running the store wouldn't be easy, but this was for her child. She would move mountains for this baby.

That morning, after making sure Jared would be preoccupied with talking to store employees about the practical joker, she'd set everything up. Now she had only to find Jared and start his reformation.

And that was exactly what had her palms sweating and her heart doing the jitterbug. Because when he began to resist—and he would resist—he might leave Quiet Brook.

Finding him was the easy part. He was talking to one of the clerks at the customer service desk. As she hung back, the woman, Marcia, leaned across the counter, clutched Jared's sleeve and gave him a sweet smile.

Just as everyone in the store had been invited to her wedding by her proud father, everyone in the store also knew that she had been back in Quiet Brook without Jared for months now. Anyone with a smattering of common sense could figure out that Jared was or soon would be free for the taking. Much as she couldn't exactly blame Marcia for trying to snare Jared's attention, she didn't particularly need to watch some other woman succeeding with Jared where she had failed, so she went right ahead and interrupted.

It only took her a few seconds to get Jared away from Marcia and down a store aisle. She didn't really feel guilty, either. What she had to do with him today was far more important than his getting a date. If he wanted Marcia in the future, he'd know where to find her. But somehow, she thought, suppressing a grim smile, she hoped he would be too involved in playing dad to their baby.

"Were you busy?"

His lips curled with a glimmer of amusement as he studied her, trying to figure out what she was up to. "I was in the middle of trying to find this Grinch for you, so yes, I guess you could say that."

"I was wondering if you'd like to help me out with something."

"I thought that was what I was doing." He leaned his elbows back against the edge of one of the counters and watched her, those darned dark blue eyes wary again. If she was to get him to come with her, she would have to throw him off guard.

Getting a sudden inspiration, she reached up and straightened the collar of his blue-and-black flannel shirt. Her fingertips brushed against his skin almost of their own accord.

That got him. Straightening, he gently took her hand and lowered it back down away from him, which she had expected he'd do. What she didn't expect was that he'd hold it for a few seconds longer than he really had to before he let it go.

"What's on your mind?" he asked.

"I want us to be alone for a while."

The responding interest in his eyes was total reflex, Shea realized, but still, a gentle longing for that look to be real threaded through her and tied her up in a knot. The physical chemistry between them was still there, probably always would be. But sadly, without mutual understanding and the fulfillment of each other's emotional needs, there would never be the everlasting love between them that she craved. She could have sworn they'd almost had it—before she'd asked him for a child.

"Alone how?" he asked, snapping her out of her reverie.

"Completely alone and undisturbed—with you. To work out some of this…tension we've been under." Carefully, she lifted her hand back up and ran her finger along his shoulder to his collarbone against the soft flannel of his shirt.

Jared stiffened, not really wanting her to touch him

but unable to bring himself, one more time, to take her hand away. He hated holding back from Shea, trying to be an impenetrable wall so that she would go away and seek the happiness he couldn't give her. He was tired of not being able to hold her in his arms. Too damned tired of it all—but he had no choice. He had to let her go.

Or make her leave him alone—for her own good.

"You're not trying to start something you can't finish, are you?" he asked quietly.

Seeing the warning in his eyes, Shea swallowed and backed off. There was catching a man off guard, and then there was putting her heart in harm's way. She was dangerously closer to the second than the first.

"Will you come with me?" she asked before she lost her courage and ran. "Please? You'll only be gone a couple of hours at most, and I promise you the experience of a lifetime."

Jared didn't know what to think. Shea had always been straightforward with him, but he couldn't believe, with the divorce so close, that she was inviting him to be alone with her for the obvious reason. So why? It couldn't be just to talk about their divorce. Even if she wanted to drop the proceedings by claiming she no longer wanted to have a family, he wouldn't let her do that. In time, she'd come to regret that decision and only end up hating him.

"Yeah, I'll go." This new side of her had him so puzzled he figured it would be worth wasting a couple of hours to go along with her—as long as he remembered to stay nothing more than a casual observer.

No matter what she wanted.

"The woods?" Jared remarked as Shea parked her father's pickup on the edge of a broad expanse of pine trees about five miles outside of Quiet Brook. He watched her take the keys out, put them in her pants pocket and open the door. "From the way you were talking, I was certain you'd take that turn going out to the hotel on the interstate."

"Wishful thinking, Jared?" Shea asked with a subdued grin, even though her heart was a lump in her throat with the question. Sitting so close to him for even the short ride out there had her remembering all the times she had lain in bed in his arms, thinking that the world was hers to have and to hold. Pushing those thoughts aside, she got out of the truck, then turned around to look at him. He was watching her intently. Just to give him something more to think about, she added, "Actually, a nice warm hotel would be cozy, but it would ruin the experience."

"So where *are* we going to have this experience, Shea?" he asked, sounding halfway between amused and cautious.

"Out there," she said, gesturing with her hand to the greenery several yards away.

"It's too cold out there. It'll never work."

Feeling almost giddy with worry about what was to come, Shea couldn't resist the banter. "You could always make it work anywhere, Jared. What happened?"

"Abstinence. I'm out of practice."

She continued to search his dark blue eyes, which

were glinting with amusement. "I guess at the rate we were going at it, a little celibacy probably did you some good."

"Gee, thanks. May I assume I'm facing more of the same now?"

"You may. Making love was *not* the reason I brought you out here."

"I knew that," he said solemnly.

Suddenly, they shared smiles that were almost as good as the first ones of discovery and intimacy, smiles that said they understood each other again, something Shea hadn't thought was possible. Maybe, her heart told her, just maybe, he wouldn't be as upset about her news as she'd imagined.

Leaning down to reach behind the seat, she lifted up the ax she'd left there, backed away, shut her door and rounded the truck to open his. He sat there without moving, regarding her and the ax with shaded eyes.

"I brought you out here to show you some Christmas spirit." Giving him a warm smile from her heart, she took a deep breath and blew out frosted air. "We, Jared, are going to cut down a Christmas tree—together."

"I don't have a choice?"

He wore a deep frown of disapproval that was meant to cut her off at the pass, but she was having none of it. "Jared Burroughs, you're going to absorb some Christmas spirit—if it kills you. No, you don't have a choice."

"Because you have an ax?" He grinned. "You'll

have to do better than that, sweetheart, to keep me here. An ax won't even slow me down.''

"No, but walking will," she replied sweetly, grinning widely back at him. "I have the keys to the truck.''

Taking a second to consider that, Jared gave her a long glance, and the ax a short one. "One way or the other, I guess I'm a captive audience—although wrestling those keys away from you would probably be a whole lot more fun than hunting up a Christmas tree.''

"But you won't go there, Jared." Her words were half an order and half a reminder—to herself and to him, for she was feeling a delicious ache at the very idea of his hands all over her body. Such traitorous thoughts she did not need right now. Over was over.

Seemingly giving in, he got out of the truck and slammed the door. With a nod, he indicated the masses of pines to the north. "I assume this is someone's land?''

"McCrory's Tree Farm," she said cheerfully. "Dad trades a tree for a gift certificate from Denton's every year. Usually the two of us come out when we're ready and find the perfect tree together.''

But this year was different. This year, she'd worked it out so that choosing the family Christmas tree would hold a very special meaning, which was why Jared *had* to be there.

Jared didn't want to participate in this with Shea, and he leaned back against the truck, trying to figure out how he could make her understand that. The joy of Christmas glowed in Shea's eyes and flushed her cheeks pink. She was having fun at the very thought of choosing a tree. On the other hand, if he went with her, he would only end up saying something that would knock all the spirit right out of her, because he didn't come close to knowing what that feeling was that made cutting down a tree for her living room such an event for her. He could have been about to pick tomatoes at the supermarket for all he cared.

"I'll wait here." He stared straight at her, knowing there would be an argument.

After setting the ax on the bed of the truck, she went over to him and took his hands in hers. Even after being out in the cold, her hands were warm, just like the smile lighting her face.

"Sorry, you're not getting off so easily. I need you to come with me."

"Hell, Shea, I'll only ruin it for you—"

She lifted a finger to his lips to make him stop talking. "No, you won't," she said. "As long as you're with me, you won't. I promise."

She had a look in her eyes that told him she wanted this with all her heart, and suddenly he realized that he was unable to deny her something as simple as a tree when he had already denied her a child.

"All right."

She glowed with pleasure. Grabbing his hand and the ax, she pulled him with her toward the dirt path worn by many years of Christmas trees being dragged to cars.

"I usually try to pick a seven footer," she told him. "The more majestic, the better."

He didn't want to say anything that would dampen

her pleasure, so he trailed behind her, keeping his silence. Taking a deep breath, he found himself noticing the smell of pine for the first time since he could remember.

"What do you look for in a tree?" she asked as they reached the first stand of pine.

"I've never had this particular pleasure," he said, choosing his words carefully.

"No tree farms around you, hmm?" Shea commented, giving him a sideways glance without being obvious about it. He wasn't saying much, but he didn't seem to be irritated, either. That was good. Feeling a little more hopeful about this plan of hers, she ventured on to fill the silence and keep the mood merry. "I don't think buying from a lot is as much fun," she told him. "You don't get a true impression of a tree until it's been standing for a couple of hours, but by that time, you've already paid for it and it's too late. Can't get the perfect tree that way."

Which was what she was after. Surveying the tree in front of her, Shea knew it wasn't right for what she had planned.

"I wouldn't know about lot trees, either," Jared said idly from behind her. "I've never gone Christmas tree hunting before."

"Your father always picked yours out?" Shea asked, keeping her voice as nonchalant as she could, even though she was excited. They were making progress. Jared had once told her enough about his childhood for her to know he hadn't been happy and that he'd grown up on a farm with his dad and an aunt who'd died when he was a child. He'd never gone into particulars, saying that he'd rather leave the past alone and live from day to day.

In order not to overwhelm him with her interest in his childhood that might shut him up again, Shea tried to keep her eyes on the trees, although she was very aware that Jared was never far behind her. She walked toward a pine that looked promising, only to find on closer inspection that one side had stunted branches. No good. Her tree had to perfect.

"No, I mean we never had a tree in the house."

"No tree? How sad!" She turned abruptly to look at him, and the ax in her hand caught and shaved some of the pine needles off one of the fuller branches of the tree next to her.

"There's a pine that will never be the same again," Jared said dryly. A second later, he was reaching out and taking the ax from her. "How about letting me carry that, before I say something that really catches you—or me—by surprise?"

"You might have a point," she said, looking at the damage she'd done, and then turning her thoughts back to what was really important—the Christmasizing of Jared. He was so close to her again, and the scent of his aftershave was mingling with the scent of the pines, weaving a spell around her. She swallowed. "You never had a tree, not even one time? You never told me that."

"It's not important."

Reaching up, she caught the edges of his open jacket and stared into his eyes, wanting him to understand. "Everything about you is important."

He didn't move, and neither did she. She gazed at

him, melting inside, wanting to kiss him, wanting him to kiss her, to be husband and wife again...but always, always, aware of the lingering pain caused by knowing that their marriage was so unfixable that a true reconciliation would be impossible.

Never releasing the light hold she had on his jacket, she continued to look up at him. "I won't push—but I do care. Please, talk to me."

For a minute longer, he continued to look down at her. And then, suddenly, the words started coming.

"My father didn't celebrate *any* holidays, Shea," he said, his eyes going distant with the memory. "From what my aunt told me, he'd never had much interest in them, but then when my mother died, anything that was a celebration just stopped. No Easter bunny or candy, no Christmas tree, and no presents. Dad didn't allow even my aunt to bring gifts. Claimed it would spoil me."

"How terrible," she said, her heart going out to the child Jared had been. No wonder he never found any joy in anything; never seemed awash in happiness. The thought of Jared as a little boy, hoping for a Santa Claus and presents that never came, made her grip his jacket tighter, holding the material the way she wanted to hold him. But she didn't have the right. His intense gaze, now focused on her hands, told her that. Feeling horribly sad, she dropped her hands to her sides. "I'm so sorry, Jared. But why not celebrate the holiday now? You've said yourself that the past is over."

"I know." He shrugged. "I don't see the sense in

it, I guess. It's all pretty commercial and fake anyway.''

It seemed commercial and fake because he didn't feel the joy and love in the season, and that made her eyes brim with tears.

"Aw, Shea," he said gently, "don't cry for me." He reached up to brush an escaping tear from her cheek. "That's why I didn't want to come out here with you. I've gone and wrecked what should have been a happy trip."

"No, you haven't," she insisted. "I'm all right." She was just crying for the little boy Jared had been, waiting for a Santa who never came, and for Jared's child, who would wait all its life for a daddy who would also never come.

The tears had to stop, she told herself. She was supposed to be helping him have *fun*.

Needing to end this topic of conversation so that she could pull her tumultuous emotions together, she swiped at her eyes with her jacket sleeve. "Let's get back to work," she said as jovially as she could.

As she pretended to turn her attention back to the trees and continued going through the rows of pines, her thoughts remained on Jared. She'd hoped what she had planned for that morning would soften his heart some, but now she realized that she was going to need a miracle to change him—a true Christmas miracle called love.

Love that couldn't come from her. She didn't want to trust whatever feelings she had for him enough to ever call them love again. The huge barrier of their different expectations still stood squarely between them. So where on earth was she going to find the miracle of love to break through to him?

It was the stillness more than anything that disrupted her thoughts at that moment. Nothing was stirring, and she no longer sensed Jared's presence nearby. Thinking he had returned to the truck to wait, she headed back the way she'd come, and it was then she realized she heard chopping noises. Frowning, she followed the sound until she found him.

He was chopping down the tree with the stunted and now partially shaved branches.

"I don't want that tree."

Swinging again, he ignored her.

"It's got a bad side."

"Don't we all."

Two more chops, and Shea felt her frustration grow. Her plan was falling apart, and she had to stop the downward spiral before it got any worse.

"Jared, it's not a perfect tree. I'm not keeping it."

As soon as he finished pushing the tree over, Jared dropped the ax to the ground, straightened and skewered her with a grin that made her tingle to her toes despite the fact that the tree he had chosen was not the most perfect one in the world and that that would wreck everything.

"You see, Shea," he said in a tone that she'd never heard from him before, somewhere between persuasive and lecturing, "that's always been your problem. You've never understood that perfection can be in the eye of the beholder. Like this tree, for instance. Sure, it's got a couple of flaws, but it's a good, fresh tree and it should stay green through New Year's without losing its needles.''

Her head tilted as she decided what to say about *that*. ''For someone who never had a Christmas tree, you sure know a lot about them.''

''When I figured out one Christmas that Santa wasn't coming, Shea, I pretended. I got myself an encyclopedia and studied pine trees and Christmas customs. I planned for the day when I would be on my own and I would know everything about Christmas that my father didn't have the heart to teach me. That's where I learned about the perfect Christmas, Shea. From books.''

''Oh, Jared, I'm sorry,'' she managed to get out.

As much as Jared had not wanted to spoil her outing, minutes before, when she turned away from him, he'd realized he had. So he'd decided to chop down a tree—any damned tree—so he could go back to Quiet Brook, find their practical joker and get the hell out of her life before he hurt her any more. This one, with its imperfections, had all but beckoned to him.

But that was crazy, he thought. Trying to ignore the way Shea was looking at him, he picked up the ax and the bottom of the tree and silently began to drag the pine toward the clearing.

Shea followed him, feeling kind of dizzy, probably from her emotions being hung out to dry. She ought to go sit down and shut up, she supposed, but Jared had just started opening up, and she wanted to concentrate on him. The better she knew him, the better she would know what made him happy, and only then could she change him.

"Why, Jared? If you wanted Christmas so much as a child that you studied all about it, what happened to make you stop wanting it?"

"I grew up." He continued walking through the clearing toward the truck, pulling the tree behind him over the cold, hard dirt.

"Surely that wasn't the only reason you gave up on such a wonderful holiday," she said as they reached the pickup.

He waited until he'd put the ax away and hoisted the tree in the back before he turned to her. "I tried to celebrate Christmas by myself once," he told her, "and it never measured up to my dream. I figured it was because I was old enough to know there was no Santa Claus, and from that time on, it all seemed pointless, as I've said before. Christmas is for kids. I missed my chance."

"No, you didn't," she countered.

He regarded her with a look of resignation. "What do you mean?"

She took a deep breath that did nothing to stop the world from swirling around her, then plunged in. "Now that you've decided on your choice of a perfect tree, Jared, I want you to have the other part of my present. I doubt that you're ever going to look at the season in the same way again." She hoped.

"That would be a miracle." Jared wondered why her evergreen eyes held a subtle hint of worry, which was at odds with the fact that she was about to give him a present, something that should have been making her happy. He decided that whatever her gift was, he'd accept it so her holiday outing wouldn't be a total disaster. "Okay, what did you get me?"

For a split second, Jared swore she began to glow with his simple concession to accept her present. A feeling of warmth at her happiness rushed over him, but then he reminded himself of the facts, which were as cold as the chill air around them. Their differences were irreconcilable. The divorce was next week.

So simple. So painful.

"The present goes with the tree," she said, giving him a lopsided grin as she reached into her jacket pocket and pulled out a small box wrapped in white paper and tied with a red ribbon. "But, of course, you can take it home with you if you like."

Jared stared down at her hand and then into her eyes. He tried to read the message they were sending. He had a feeling that the gift was going to change something between them, but how, he had no idea.

"Look, Shea, before I open it, I'm sorry that I didn't get you anything."

"That's all right," she said softly. "It's Christmas. The joy is in the giving."

And he wanted to give her something. The only gift he could think of would tear him apart, but looking at her soft mouth, the warmth on her face and her caring eyes, he couldn't resist. Before she could protest, he carefully pulled her close and covered her mouth with his own in a Christmas kiss.

The feel of her, so familiar, so sensual, left him reeling. God help him, he'd forgotten. He savored her mouth, her lips, and gave her the kiss that he always saved just for her. Finally, when she had melted against him, kissing him back, her arms wrapped around his neck, he knew he had to stop before they both lost their senses.

Regret in his eyes, the pain already digging into his heart, he pulled back from her. He expected Shea to come to her senses, too, and do the same, but she swayed instead. She was using him for support, Jared realized. That wasn't at all like her.

"Hey," he said, drawing her back against his chest. With a sigh that sounded grateful, she leaned against him, and for a few quiet seconds they stayed like that. "You were going to faint, weren't you?" he asked, half-growling to hide his concern.

"You keep holding me this close, I still might," she whispered.

Somewhere deep in his heart, he smiled. "Have that much of an impact on you after all this time, do I?"

If he only knew the half of it. Shea's head had stopped whirling, so she gently pushed away from him, anxious to keep some distance between them and just a bit peeved that he was right—he was still rocking her off her feet whenever he touched her.

"I don't care how big an impact you have on me," she said, recovering a little. "You're still just getting this for Christmas." Taking his hand, she pushed the box into it. More swiftly than she thought he would, he lifted the lid and pulled out his gift.

It was a Christmas-tree ornament, a flat piece of silver cut in the shape of a toy train engine. Jared stared at the image stamped on it, and the cherubic child in the engine's window. Across the top was engraved, "Baby's ETA: June 15."

Baby's ETA. Estimated time of arrival. He felt the ground give way beneath his feet. Staying upright by twisting around to lean against the bed of the truck, he reread the engraving, then glanced down at the tiny gift card in the bottom of the box.

"Merry Christmas, Daddy," Shea had written.

He looked back at the ornament and formed each word silently, taking his time. But the words hadn't been a figment of his imagination and still read the same.

"I thought this could get you started with your very own set of Christmas memories that you can share with the baby when it gets a little older."

Shea's voice sounded far off, even though she was right next to him. A baby.

"I kind of wanted *Baby's First Christmas*, but I thought that should be saved for next year, when our baby is actually here. I'll make sure you get a new ornament every year, and then, when the baby's all grown with a family of his or her own, it can have the set for himself. What do you think?"

"I think," Jared said, gulping, "that maybe you'd better drive us back to town." He couldn't say anything else. Not yet.

As though it were crystal, he carefully tucked the ornament back into the box, replaced the lid, took a deep breath, turned and looked at her. Really looked at her.

She was pregnant with his child.

"How did this happen?" he asked, his voice

sounding raspy in his ears. How could it have possibly happened?

"It's the season for miracles," she told him simply.

What little breath he had left went out of him.

He looked so...so... dumbstruck that Shea took pity on him. Reaching up to clutch the bed of the truck herself, needing the support, she gave him the clinical explanation. "The doctor's exact words were, 'Even the best birth control is not foolproof.'"

For a few seconds, his eyes held hers. But all he said was, "I take full responsibility for this."

"Half," she corrected, keeping her voice level, waiting. She was sure that wasn't all he had to say, and whatever came next, she would have to keep her head and remember her goal. This was only the first hurdle, and she'd known it would not be an easy one.

"Since you were dizzy before, maybe I'd better drive instead." Jared rounded the truck and slipped behind the wheel. Shea joined him inside and put the key in the ignition. Jared wordlessly started the engine.

"We need to talk about this, Jared," she pointed out.

"If you're worried about money, don't be," he said, his voice sounding emotionless as he put the truck in gear. "I'll pay child support. Whatever you need, you and the baby will have. Clothes, a place of your own, anything—just name it."

"A daddy," she said softly. "I want the baby to have a storybook life, with a real daddy for Christmas, the kind I had."

His jaw set. He should have expected Fate had

something rotten in mind when he'd been summoned to Quiet Brook. It was Christmas after all. "I can't be that daddy you're dreaming of, Shea," he finally said.

He needed her to understand, so he broke down and told her what he should have told her at the beginning.

"Dad was never the kind of father you're talking about, Shea—a father like Mack is to you." His concentration on the road, he steered expertly around a wood plank that had dropped off someone's truck. "If I so much as asked about Santa Claus, he told me to face reality and forget about getting something for nothing. If I said I was looking forward to something, he told me not to count my chickens. It got so that it was easier just not to care at all. Once I stopped caring, I stopped feeling joy about anything for a long, long time. Then you came along." He left it at that. He had a feeling she would understand.

"Anyway, a man like Mack is what you'd be expecting for this child. I could never come close to being the kind of person Mack is, a giving man who reaches out, who enjoys everything about life." No matter how much he might have wanted to, for Shea's sake. "That's why I can't get into the whole fatherhood bit. I'm too much like my father to wish me on a kid." He paused, then carefully added, "Ever."

Shea sat next to him without moving, her eyes straight ahead, her delicate features drawn. Jared would have given his right arm not to have said that to her, to have withdrawn from the situation without saying much of anything, the way he'd done with

their marriage. But he had to make her realize that
their child deserved better for a father than a man who
was uncomfortable around kids and had no desire to
change, who didn't particularly care for things like
Christmas and no longer, if he ever had, saw the joy
in the simple things of life. That was as clear as the
air around them. He knew what kind of man he was
and could tell that he wouldn't be a good father....

So why couldn't Shea?

Chapter Five

Shea felt shaky all over. She should have known breaking through Jared's shell wouldn't be as easy as spending a couple of hours cutting down a Christmas tree, sharing some laughter and giving him a present meant to warm his heart. Her inclination was to cry her eyes out. She could go ahead and do just that— let the tears explode all over her face and all over what little relationship she still had with her unborn baby's father—or she could pull herself together and realize that she and Jared had come a long way in only one afternoon. She now knew that his father had been a tightwad with his heart, and that grim legacy had been passed down to his son.

She also knew now why Jared had clammed up and gotten remote when she'd wanted him to share his hopes and dreams with her. How could he, when he was afraid to dream—or to need—for fear of being disappointed?

It was thanks to his father that Jared had built a protective wall around himself and buried his emotions so he wouldn't care that he was missing out on the things that made life special—like family love and community traditions. Now, after learning what his life had been like as a child, she could even acknowledge that Jared's walking away from discussions about their future had probably been his way of keeping himself remote, detached. If he never let himself care, he'd never get hurt. That was what his father had taught him by denying him what every child needed—unconditional love, caring and warmth.

So what to do now? Their marriage wasn't salvageable, not when he'd have to change his whole outlook on life in order for her to be happy. But surely she could soften his heart enough for him to accept his own little baby, someone who wouldn't ask anything of him except love. Jared at least had that in him, she knew. She had felt wanted from the very beginning with him. Whether he'd wanted, loved or just needed her, she didn't know, but she believed he could give love in his own fashion. To their baby. Eventually.

She cast a surreptitious glance at him. He could have been a statue, so stiffly and silently was he sitting there, driving the truck down the road back to the main highway. The question was now, would her original plan be enough? Would giving him a Christmas to remember suffice to melt the cocoon of ice around his heart and help him feel the joys and pleasures that life offered? And could she pull off the change before Jared figured out who the Grinch was and left?

The first thing to do, she decided, clenching her jaw, was to save her tears till she was all alone in her room at night and afraid again. Her tears had always closed Jared up even more. She had to remember what her mother had been fond of saying—love and laughter would cure anything. She wished with all her heart her mother hadn't died when she was eleven. Shea had a feeling her mother would have known how to help Jared now.

Straightening up in her seat as best she could with the seat belt fastened, she pasted a resolute smile on her face and waited for him to notice it. When he stopped to turn onto the highway, he did.

"You look too happy," he said. "If I didn't know the ax was out of your reach, I'd be worried."

"I wouldn't dream of killing you, Jared, not even figuratively." Love and laughter, she told herself.

"Because killing would be too good for me, and you've decided to torture me first?"

"If I decide to torture you, I won't need an ax," she said.

The low, sweet tone of her voice as she spoke conjured up all sorts of "tortures" in Jared's mind that she could still inflict upon him. Even now, that peaceful, "wait and see" smile on her lips and the scent of her perfume were wrapping themselves around every part of him that still held life and making him vulnerable. She was having his baby....

A baby that she knew full well he didn't want.

Where was that look of serenity on her face coming from?

Tense, he drove toward Quiet Brook, wishing he was driving back to Topeka instead—alone—so he could get away from this woman who wanted nothing—and everything—to do with him.

She was having his baby.

A fine sheen of sweat broke out on his forehead. He was having a kid who wasn't ever going to know his father. He knew he couldn't have it otherwise, but it felt...terrible.

"You're going to stay on to find the Grinch, aren't you?" Shea asked. "Dad's counting on you."

"I wouldn't break a promise to Mack." Mack. He was going to be a grandfather. So was his own father—but Gil Burroughs didn't much figure into his life anymore. "Does Mack know about the baby?"

Shea's lips spread in a wide smile, and her eyes twinkled, warming him to the core just like always. "Are you kidding?" she asked. "He would have been shouting it from the rooftop of our store the second he found out. You would have heard it in Topeka before you left, and you wouldn't have been around him five seconds before he would have been patting you on the back and saying he knew you had it in you."

"He does have a way with words," Jared said, unable to resist.

She smiled. "I guess you won't want to be there when I tell him?"

"It depends, Shea." He rounded a curve, keeping his eyes on the road where it was safer—in more ways than one. "Are you going to tell him *you're* having the baby—or *we* are? If you tell him we are, he might think we had plans to stay together, and I don't think that would be fair to him."

The only sign that his question bothered her was the way she tightly balled her slender fingers on her leg until they were pale.

"I'll be happy to tell him in whatever way makes you feel the most comfortable, Jared." She gave him another careful smile.

Jared knew this wasn't going to be easy. Mack was going to look at him like he was permanent family and had hung the moon besides—never mind there were only a few days left until his and Shea's divorce became final. At the very least, his friend was going to expect the best of him.

Just like Shea did.

Well, the best would have to be that he stayed around long enough to find the Grinch, then got the hell out of Quiet Brook away from Shea and his need for her. And away from their child. Jared knew beyond a doubt the kid would be better off without him in the picture.

"After we get the tree home, we'd better return to Denton's. I need to make sure Dad isn't wearing himself out subbing for me, and you should get back to your investigation." Her eyes narrowed. "Speaking of which, aren't you worried about your business?"

Jared wasn't sure what to make of this. Shea seemed to have totally dropped all talk about their child and given up trying to persuade him to change his mind.

He would worry about that later. "Between the answering machine and the fax, I'm handling things," he said in answer to her question. "Besides, I'm not expecting this Grinch hunt to take very long. Not more than a couple of days." Pausing at the stop sign on the corner near her house, he glanced at her. "That is, barring any other time wasters you have up your sleeve for me." Just so she didn't misunderstand, he hastily amended, "Like getting the tree, I mean."

"Getting a tree was not a time waster, Jared Burroughs," she protested as he turned onto her street. "It was a way to show you some hometown Christmas spirit, and to let you know about your child as gracefully as possible."

"Yeah, well, I don't much like surprises," he said, shutting off the engine. "I hope there aren't any more in store for me here."

"Normally I'd be full of helpful responses for your comments," she said as sweetly as possible. "But right now I can only think of one."

He turned to her and waited.

"Cope." She grinned.

Her answer reminded him of their happier days, and his mouth twitched up at the edges in a trace of a smile. "Darlin', you're sounding more like my side of the family every day."

"Oh, merciful Lord, then I *have* been hanging around you too long," she said.

He groaned, and with another last grin at him, she climbed down from the truck and took her keys out of her pocket to open up the garage.

Not wanting her to bend over and lift the balky

sliding door, Jared went to her side and took the ring of keys from her hand, drawing a sudden breath at the feel of her palm against his fingers. He didn't know if he could stand even a couple more days of being around a woman he still wanted but would never have.

"So we stash the tree in the garage and then head out," Shea said, her eyes meeting his with a long look. "Can you come back here early instead of staying late at the store? You can help Dad set it up, and we'll decorate it and tell him about the baby then. Okay?"

"Yeah, if that's what you think is best." If it was up to him, he'd just go and tell Mack right now, but the baby was important to Shea, and, hell, who was he to spoil her moment?

She gave him a smile that would melt any snowman, and he warned himself to turn away and get on with the task at hand. It worked. Hoisting the tree over to one corner of the garage, he knew he also couldn't let himself think about being around his child. The baby would need a parent who could give it the wonderful childhood he'd never had—and that parent would be Shea. He would not stick around trying to fit into her perfect world here, only to end up making her life hell. He couldn't—and it hurt.

Toward seven o'clock that evening, Shea put a plate of iced Christmas-tree cookies on the coffee table and grinned at Jared and her father as they stepped back from the tree. The two men had been together since Jared had arrived, working at chopping the bottom of the tree to fit the stand, and now that it was up, looking it over carefully. While she couldn't tell if Jared was having fun, he was at least *involved*. And he'd shown up. Somewhere inside her, her baby latched onto a little star of hope.

"A beautiful tree." Mack surveyed it with a discerning eye and a nod of approval. "Jared says you chose it in less than ten minutes?" He chuckled. "That has to be a record in decisiveness for you."

"Yes, well, Jared convinced me that the tree's flaws gave it character."

Her father frowned. "What flaws?"

"The branches."

Her father lifted his eyebrows as though he had no idea what Shea was referring to. Frowning, she walked over to the tree, peeked around the back and then to either side. Knowing full well that the tree should appear a tad hollow somewhere because of the stunted branches and the damage she'd done to it, she shot Jared a questioning look.

"What happened to my tree?"

"Your tree?" he countered, reminding her with an ironic grin that she hadn't liked the tree at all. "Maybe the Grinch stole it." He shrugged his shoulders and asked, "What's the big deal? He left another one in its place."

Shea caught a glint of something mischievous in Jared's eyes—just like the good old days.

"Besides, Shea," he continued, "this one is *perfect*."

His emphasis on that last word was not lost on her.

He was behind this tree switch, not any Grinch, but the question was, why?

She wasn't even sure she wanted to know, but she did want her tree back. She'd spent the rest of the afternoon in her office thinking about that flawed tree and its significance. It was the first tree that Jared had picked out ever, and she'd decided her baby's ornament belonged on it. It was only right.

And Jared had changed it. She didn't know whether to laugh or cry. No, she did know. Love and laughter.

Humbug.

"I want my tree back."

Her shocked father stared from her determined face to Jared's closed-off one, then did the only logical thing—retreated, mumbling about getting some ornaments from the garage. Jared started to follow, but Shea snagged his sleeve with her fingers.

"Uh-huh. You're staying here." Waiting just long enough to hear the back door open to be sure her father was well outside, she asked, "Where's my tree?"

"*Your* tree?" Jared was incredulous, spreading his hands out wide. "But you hated that tree."

"That was hours ago. In the meantime, I decided differently. What happened to it?"

"In the meantime, I decided differently," he repeated in a suffering, but teasing, tone. "You've never changed your mind this fast before. You used to make a choice and stick with it forever. Maybe it's the pregnancy that's changing you. I sure hope it is because then I could believe you aren't doing this to make me crazy."

"I'm the one who's starting to feel a little crazy here, Jared," she said warningly, taking a couple of steps closer to him. "Where's my tree?"

His eyes twinkled as he stood his ground. "Why is it so important for you to suddenly have a tree you hated six hours ago?"

"It's a totally sentimental reason you would just roll your eyes over."

He considered that for a second or two, rubbing his teeth against his bottom lip. "Try me. Why do you suddenly want an imperfect tree in the middle of your perfect Quiet Brook Christmas?"

She wanted to say it would never again be a perfect Christmas without him, but she couldn't, no matter how much being this near to him enticed her senses. She wanted to curl up in his arms on a rug in front of a fireplace, but her only alternative was to stand there and explain what had occurred to her that afternoon.

"I spent a lot of time thinking about this, and..." Her words drifted off as she tried to choose the right words so he would understand. "It's the first tree you ever picked out, and when you hung that ornament I gave you on it, I guess I thought it would be the beginning of a tradition for our baby that I could always tell it about. The Christmas its daddy chopped down the tree for its very own ornament. It would have been...perfect."

That single word hung in the air between them.

"I'm sorry, Shea. I never thought to look at it that way. I ruined it for you, didn't I?"

He looked sadder, Shea thought, than when she'd

told him she was divorcing him. That wasn't good. She was trying to *help* him, not make everything worse. And for that reason, she knew she had to lie.

"You didn't ruin a thing," she told him, even though she knew in her heart the picture-perfect pine inches away wouldn't be the same. "You tried to make me happy with a better tree. That was really nice. Forget it. We have this one." She gave him a weak smile. "I love it."

"You never were a great liar." After regarding her for another minute, he leaned forward and grabbed her hand. His expression never changing, he pulled her toward the kitchen. "C'mon."

Because she had no choice, she followed him right into the kitchen where the aroma of oranges she'd brought home was mingling with the cinnamon of the sugar cookies that were still cooling on the rack. Mack had deposited two medium-size cardboard boxes on the floor and next to them was testing a string of fat, old-fashioned Christmas lights for burnouts.

"Good. You two are just in time to start hanging the ornaments," he said, pointing toward the boxes.

Letting go of her hand, Jared stepped around the lights and reached for his coat hanging by the rear door. "No decorating tonight, Mack," he said, pulling on his jacket.

He was leaving? Shea stared at him, confused.

"What do you mean, no decorating tonight?" Mack asked, plugging in the string. "I thought that's why you came back here early instead of spending the evening at the store."

Shea watched as the floor lit up in bright colors, giving a false gaiety to the scene. Feeling miserable for having driven Jared away, Shea could only stare at her almost ex-husband.

"Shea and I have something we have to do." Jared took her coat off the hook, stepped around the lights again and handed it to her as he headed back into the living room. "You'll need to hurry, though, Shea. I'm not sure how much time we have."

"To do what?" she asked, following him, aware her father was trailing along after them both. She was filled with relief that Jared wasn't retreating again— not exactly anyway. But then she only grew more confused as Jared neared the tree, reached into the branches and lifted the whole thing up, stand and all.

"Hey!" Mack said. "Where are you going with our tree?"

"Sorry, Mack, I need it. I'm going to try to retrieve Shea's perfect Christmas tradition that I gave away," Jared said. "To do that, we'll have to trade trees." He moved the tree to the front door, which he opened with his free hand, then he stopped long enough to glance over his shoulder at her. "Are you coming?"

A glad feeling like Shea had never had before filled every inch of her. Yanking on her coat, she started doing up buttons. Because Jared didn't *have* to go after that tree, it was, she thought, perhaps the nicest thing he had ever done for her. She wasn't even going to question it.

"Did I miss something here?" Mack asked, looking from Jared to her. "Why on earth isn't this tree good enough?"

"Because its branches aren't stunted and shaved," Shea said, buttoning her last button and shoving on her gloves.

As she hurried toward the door, she stopped for a second and took in the sight of her father raking his fingers through his salt-and-pepper hair in confusion.

"By the way," she said, her voice filled with happiness, "I thought you might like to know, since we could be a while and we were going to tell you this evening anyway—"

"Know what?"

"You're going to be a grandfather."

"Very funny," Mack said, shaking his head and rolling his eyes as though he thought she was kidding. "Kids."

"Honestly, Dad, I'm having Jared's baby," she said.

Smiling widely, she slipped outside and shut the door behind her. If she knew her father the way she thought she did, she and Jared needed to get going fast or they'd never shake loose of Mack Denton this evening.

She hurried down the walk to the truck just as Jared was opening the door on the driver's side. It was his turn to be perplexed as she slipped into the seat and counted, "Three, two, one..."

The front door jerked open and Mack's voice exploded into the evening air. "Shea Denton Burroughs, you're what?"

"I'm coming back soon, Dad!" she called. "We'll discuss it then."

"I'll be waiting, and, Jared, you'd better come back with her!"

"Yes, sir." Jared climbed into the truck and gave her a look that said he was glad they were leaving.

She grinned at him. "Told you you would have heard the news in Topeka."

Chuckling, Jared shook his head and became serious. "Do you think that's wise, telling him right before we leave? News like that could give a man a heart attack." He lowered his voice and said, almost to himself, "Believe me, I know."

"I have a way of getting to people, don't I?" Shea bit back her smile, remembering she had told him that Mack was worse off than he was in order to convince Jared to stick around in Quiet Brook. "Dad looked worried about what was going on, and I wanted to leave him with a smile and something pleasant to think about."

A doubtful look on his face, Jared peered past her to the front door to see if her news had worked. Mack still stood on the front porch, arms folded across his chest. And sure enough—he was also grinning from ear to ear.

"My tree is in the store?" Shea asked as Jared pulled into the parking lot behind Denton's. Half-empty, and it was only seven-thirty in the evening, with hardly any shopping days left till Christmas. She would hazard a guess that most of the shoppers with children were walking the mall that evening while their children saw Santa. She had to do something about that, and fast. But first, the tree—for tradition's sake. "My tree is in the store?"

"Not exactly." Jared got out and rounded the truck to open her door. He had refused to tell her any details on the short ride over, saying it would be easier just to show her about the tree. She wasn't sure she understood, but she trusted him. She hadn't always liked what he had to say, but he always had very logical reasons behind whatever he did.

Which was why they weren't together, she reflected as she stepped out onto the gravel, the frosty air nipping her cheeks. He took her hand, and she followed, thinking about how much she liked having her hand nestled inside his big one and traipsing around with him to wherever.

But she shouldn't think about what she liked and didn't like about Jared while he was there in Quiet Brook. If she did, she might start believing anything was possible again, and that would not be a good idea.

The sudden realization that they were not going into the back entrance of the store startled her out of her treacherous thinking. What on earth was Jared up to that he was taking her to her tree in, of all places, the alley?

Letting go of her hand, Jared pulled a flashlight out of his pocket, clicked it on and scanned the outside wooden wall of the building. There was nothing even faintly resembling a tree resting there, and an apologetic look appeared on his face.

"I'm too late," he told her. "She must have gotten someone to take the tree to her house."

"Who?" she asked.

"Your little friend, Molly, about five years old, sandy hair. She said she knew you. Maybe she's still in the building. I saw her a couple of times this morning while I was interviewing employees, and then again this afternoon when she started talking to me. She has this annoying habit of disappearing before I can ask her where her parents are. I think she must live nearby." Turning before Shea could reply, Jared headed toward the back door of the store and held it open for her. "If we find her, maybe we can get her mom to trade trees. Since you know her and the store, where do you think a kid who spends a lot of time here might hang out?"

Shea stared at him. Jared had just given a tree to a child he didn't even know? She slipped inside, nodded at the security guard they'd employed part-time for the evening hours ever since the day they'd been robbed—the day she'd met Jared—and then turned directly in front of Jared to stop him from barreling ahead through the store.

"I have one or two ideas where children might hide," she said, "but there's one problem about all this."

"I thought you wanted to get your tree back," he said, running his hand through his dark brown hair in obvious exasperation.

"I do." Pulling down the hood of her coat, Shea stared up at him in total bewilderment. "The problem is, I have no idea who you're talking about."

Chapter Six

"What do you mean you don't know who I'm talking about? The child said—" Jared abruptly stopped speaking. What had Molly said? Just that she had seen Shea, not that she personally knew her.

They moved out of the way as a lone shopper left with a single bag, the security guard walking her outside.

"Start from the beginning," Shea suggested.

He told her of their first meeting, leaving out the part Molly had said about Shea almost crying. "Today, while I was interviewing store employees, she popped up out of nowhere and told me that this 'real' Santa of hers needed a tree." He shrugged. "I figured she was making it up and probably meant her own family. She doesn't look like her folks have much."

She nodded for him to continue.

"I knew you hated the tree I picked out, so I told

the kid that in about an hour, I'd put a tree in the alley with her name on it. That's when she told me her name. Molly 'Claus.' Obviously, the kid is heavy into this Christmas fantasy.''

"Obviously." Shea had to smile. Jared looked so skeptical, but he'd helped Molly anyway.

"Then I told her to have her dad or mom there to pick up the tree so no one else would take it. I figured I would wait there and talk to them about their kid going up to total strangers. Then I had to move out of the way for a clerk, and when I turned around, Molly had disappeared. Since I still had your keys, I went back to your garage and got your tree."

"And?"

"Nobody showed in the alley, so I left the tree there and got you another one."

He'd been worried about her Christmas. Shea couldn't help but give him a big, knowing smile.

His face taking on a cautious look, Jared backed up and sent a warning look her way. "Shea, I was just using common sense in a rough world. The kid's been going up to total strangers and offering to take them off to meet this mythical Santa. That isn't safe. The right thing to do, I figured, was to get her a tree so she wouldn't ask anyone else, and then to get someone to look after her. Since she chose me to approach, I felt responsible. That's all it was. Don't read anything else into it, okay?''

"Sorry, Jared," she said, lowering her chin to her chest as though she were a child being admonished, trying hard not to grin.

He regarded her reaction solemnly until he finally

felt like smiling, too. "You never give up, do you? You're so determined to find the good in me, aren't you?"

"No, Jared," Shea said softly, her expression turning serious. "I'm just determined to help you see the good in yourself."

For the first time, Jared wondered if he could pretend to feel all the things he knew he was supposed to be feeling—the love of holidays and the need for tradition...the need for a family. Could he? When he was a kid, he'd made up a family, with a mother who laughed at his jokes and a father who played ball with him in the backyard. When he eventually realized it wasn't going to happen, he'd buried that desire deep, so deep he no longer felt anything but an emptiness.

He had to get out of there. Find the tree, then find the Grinch...then find his way back to Topeka. He wished it sounded more appealing.

"We need to see if Molly is still around," he told her.

Shea had been watching Jared for so long she had almost forgotten why they were back at the store.

"The tree!" If she could get her tree back, it would be almost a sign that there was hope for this Christmas to be something more than a holiday of misery. Unbuttoning her coat, she hurriedly hung it on the empty coat rack near the door meant for the customers. "You think she's still somewhere inside, even though the tree's gone?"

"You never can tell."

"Let's split up, then," she suggested. "I'll ask the clerks about her, and you can start checking under the counters and behind booths, places where kids might like to hide. If you see her, yell your head off and I'll come running.''

''I'd rather stick with you.''

''If only,'' she said wistfully, but he didn't seem to hear.

Where anything connected to the little girl was concerned, they ran into a pattern of cautious denials that sounded suspicious to Shea, although for the life of her, she couldn't figure out what anyone could be hiding. When she caught reflected in the security mirror a surreptitiously given ''everything's okay'' sign sent from one employee they'd just finished interviewing to another, she knew she was right.

''They're hiding something,'' Shea whispered to Jared as they crossed the floor to a quiet area. He took her hand. Shea was sure he did it unconsciously and tried not to imagine that it meant anything at all.

But still...

''Yeah, I noticed that, too,'' Jared told her.

''Question is, what do we do?''

''Leave it to me.'' His eyes caught hers and held them, and then, with a quick squeeze of her hand, he headed toward the clerk they had just finished questioning.

Watching him talk to the employee, Shea fervently prayed for the strength to keep up her campaign to change Jared. All the signs were there that he really did want to be a part of the holiday. Take this little Molly. He'd gotten the child a tree out of the goodness of his heart, whether he wanted to acknowledge he had a heart or not. And that, of course, would be the trick—making him understand that he did.

Standing there, listening to the Christmas carol over the music system her father had installed, she saw one clerk summon another over to where Jared and she were standing. When Jared turned, Shea was surprised to see the clerk move out from behind her booth and return with him. Grace Corwin was one of her father's longtime employees, one whom Mack really trusted.

"Shea, do you know an employee named Lucy Millstone?" Jared asked.

"Lucy Millstone..." As she made one more visual sweep of the store for a little sandy-haired girl, she thought about the name and then shook her head. "It's possible Dad might have hired someone part-time in the past couple of days, but I don't know why he would have—not with the business having dropped off some." And she'd been in and out of the store since Jared's arrival, not really paying attention to faces.

"Go ahead, Grace," Jared prompted.

"Well, Mrs. Burroughs," the gray-haired woman said, wringing her hands as though she was nervous, "after your father hired Lucy, I put her to work learning the ropes. This little girl you're looking for sounds exactly like Lucy's daughter." She paused. "Please don't be mad, but with school out for the holidays, Lucy couldn't afford a sitter. We've been letting her daughter stay in the store, and whenever anyone asked about her, we act like she doesn't exist. But when Mr. Burroughs here said there might be some

WELCOME TO THE
CASINO!

Try your luck at the Roulette Wheel ...
Play a hand of Twenty-One!

How to play:

1. Play the Roulette and Twenty-One scratch-off games, as instructed on the opposite page, to see that you are eligible for FREE BOOKS and a FREE GIFT!

2. Send back the card and you'll receive TWO brand-new Silhouette Romance® novels. These books have a cover price of $3.50 each, but they are yours to keep absolutely free.

3. There's no catch. You're under no obligation to buy anything. We charge nothing — ZERO — for your first shipment. And you don't have to make any minimum number of purchases — not even one!

4. The fact is, thousands of readers enjoy receiving books by mail from the Silhouette Reader Service™ before they're available in stores. They like the convenience of home delivery, and they love our discount prices!

5. We hope that after receiving your free books you'll want to remain a subscriber. But the choice is yours — to continue or cancel, any time at all!

So why not take us up on our invitation, with no risk of any kind. You'll be glad you did!

Play Twenty-One For This Exquisite Free Gift!

THIS SURPRISE MYSTERY GIFT COULD BE YOURS FREE WHEN YOU PLAY
TWENTY-ONE

It's fun, and we're giving away *FREE GIFTS* to all players!

PLAY ROULETTE!

Scratch the silver to see where the ball has landed—7 RED or 11 BLACK makes you eligible for TWO FREE romance novels!

PLAY TWENTY-ONE!

Scratch the silver to reveal a winning hand! Congratulations, you have Twenty-One. Return this card promptly and you'll receive a fabulous free mystery gift, along with your free books!

Please send me all the free Silhouette Romance® books and the gift for which I qualify! I understand that I am under no obligation to purchase any books, as explained on the back of this card.

Name (please print clearly)

Address   Apt.#

City   State   Zip

The Silhouette Reader Service™ — Here's how it works:

Accepting free books places you under no obligation to buy anything. You may keep the books and gift and return the shipping statement marked "cancel." If you do not cancel, about a month later we'll send you 6 additional novels and bill you just $2.90 each, plus 25¢ delivery per book and applicable sales tax, if any.* That's the complete price — and compared to cover prices of $3.50 each — quite a bargain! You may cancel at any time, but if you choose to continue, every month we'll send you 6 more books, which you may either purchase at the discount price...or return to us and cancel your subscription.

*Terms and prices subject to change without notice. Sales tax applicable in N.Y.

If offer card is missing write to: Silhouette Reader Service, 3010 Walden Ave., P.O. Box 1867, Buffalo, NY 14240-9952

BUSINESS REPLY MAIL

FIRST-CLASS MAIL   PERMIT NO. 717   BUFFALO NY

POSTAGE WILL BE PAID BY ADDRESSEE

SILHOUETTE READER SERVICE
3010 WALDEN AVE
PO BOX 1867
BUFFALO NY   14240-9952

NO POSTAGE
NECESSARY
IF MAILED
IN THE
UNITED STATES

heads rolling if that little girl isn't found, I got scared for my job—which I need.''

Heads rolling? Shea quirked an eyebrow at Jared. "We definitely have to do something about your Christmas spirit.''

He grinned unabashedly. "Look at it this way. Even Santa Claus probably has to rein in the elves sometimes, right?''

"Hmm.'' She'd have to give that one some thought. Turning back to Grace, she asked, "Are the two here now?''

Grace shook her head. "Lucy said they had a Christmas pageant to go to this evening.'' She rattled off the address of the church, which was a modest one in Shea's part of town. "I really hope no one is going to get in trouble over this, Mrs. Burroughs. Lucy's an older widow, and she needs this job really bad.''

"Don't worry.'' Thanking and waving Grace on back to work, Shea said to Jared, "I strongly suggest that Santa Claus wouldn't threaten anyone. I think he'd offer praise and encouragement to his employees.'' She smiled. "And lots of bonus Christmas cookies.''

The edges of Jared's lips turned into a smile. "I wish the world was that good, Shea. But not everyone understands sweetness and light.''

"Like you.'' She gave him a tight smile and started toward the back of the store and her coat. He moved to her side.

"That's right,'' he said. "Like me.''

"I still say the kind way is the best way.''

He didn't answer. Shea hadn't really expected him to. She would just keep trying, that was all. They hadn't found the Grinch yet, so she still had some time to help Jared—for their baby's sake.

She could almost picture the little one to come. It would have dark hair, like her and Jared, and blink up at her with Jared's eyes, and coo at her with tiny lips...and dang it all, it would spend lots of time in its daddy's arms. She'd see to it.

Rounding a corner by the magazine rack, Shea found Mr. Griswold, her neighbor, who was coming from the rear of the store, his coat still on, his hat in his hand.

"Merry Christmas, Mr. Griswold," she said to the older man. "Out shopping for gifts?"

"No, no, not right now." Griswold hesitated. "Is your father around?"

"No, he's at home. You didn't notice the lights were all on when you left?"

"Naw," Griswold said, the word accompanied by a shake of his free hand in the air. His hat glimmered with a few new-fallen snowflakes that were still melting. At the sight of them, Shea grinned. The first snow of the year. It was a sign.

"It's snowing—how nice!"

"If you like hazardous driving and pain-in-the-neck shoveling, it's nice," Jared replied.

"Going soft on us, Jared?" Shea asked, her eyes twinkling. "Maybe we can find you a nice sit-down job around here, something that will keep you out of the snow."

Jared's eyes glinted as he caught on, and he grinned back. "Don't even think about it."

"Now, now, children." Mr. Griswold looked at them both, and it was then Shea noticed that his face seemed awash in misery. "Squabbling isn't good. Take it from me. It just isn't good."

"What's wrong, Mr. Griswold?" Shea asked.

"Nothing you can help with." His jaw jutted, and he sighed. "As long as I'm here, I guess I'll just go have some coffee. Maybe I'll come by again tomorrow." With a goodbye wave, he continued on his way.

"Mr. Griswold doesn't look very happy," Jared said suddenly, watching the elderly man walk away. "Does he have a family?"

"A lovely wife and a grandchild they're raising," Shea replied. She went over to the coat rack, found her coat and slipped it on. "Mr. Griswold and his friends like to come here to have coffee together at the snack bar while they talk or read the paper." Her mouth twisted in a grin, and she followed him outside into the parking lot, her shoes crunching the gravel as she walked. "Also, whenever Mr. Griswold has a fight with his wife, he comes here, finds Dad and harps about women."

"Gee, I wonder if they want company...."

"Very funny," she said sweetly, stopping and swinging around to face him. She gave him a gentle poke on the chest with her finger as snowflakes dusted them both. "Do you have a new woman you need to gripe about? I know you aren't referring to *me*."

"No new women for me, princess," he said, grabbing her finger and holding it for a long minute, warm skin against warm skin in the frosty air. "You're too unforgettable."

His words were everything she could have wished for a few months before, and now, they were just painful. Her face fell. "I know things are kind of impossible between us, but I truly want you to be happy, Jared," she said in a low voice. "I really do."

Snowflakes settled in her hair like diamonds, and Jared almost lifted his hand to brush them away. Then he remembered she wasn't his to touch.

"Don't worry about me, Shea. I'll survive." *Maybe* he would. Looking at her delicate features and remembering her warm smiles, he was no longer so sure he could go on without her laughter. Inside, he wanted to shut down. Outwardly, he wished he could escape. Once the divorce went through, it would all be over.

Reaching up, she cupped his cheek and rubbed her thumb against the dark stubble of his light beard. His hand caught hers and held it, and for one precious second, he looked so intensely at her she thought he might kiss her again, which wasn't what she wanted. Or was it? She no longer knew.

"We can't go backward, Shea."

His husky words took care of her having to come up with an answer to her own question of what she wanted, and she nodded. He was right, of course. They shouldn't be trying to go backward; they should be building a new relationship for their child's sake. Even Jared could see that.

Dropping her hand back to her side, she continued

on toward the truck, frustration breaking through her pain over his not wanting a child in the first place. Frustration, pain and grief. They should have lived happily ever after. This wasn't right. As soon as he found the Grinch, he was leaving, the divorce would go through, and...and she'd be as miserable as she'd been without him.

She'd never find anyone like Jared, she knew. Never. Real, enduring love was not something you got over, even if that love had never been in the cards.

"So we find Molly and her mom and get the tree back," she said, ignoring her pain and choosing, instead, to be strong. She had a Christmas to prepare for after all, for the town, for Jared and the baby, and for the sake of tradition. "That is, if you're still with me."

A dozen seconds passed as Jared stood silently by the front of the truck. Finally, to Shea's relief, he nodded. "I'm not sure why it's so important, but yeah—let's go after that tree."

The church could have been any old church. What stopped Jared in his tracks, though, were the twinkling Christmas lights strung all along the west side of the building and around the windows and doors.

"This place is lit up like a..." Words failed him.

"Christmas tree?" Shea suggested. She grinned when Jared mugged a frown at her. "It's for the kids, Jared."

Jared was grinning inside, actually enjoying this great Christmas-tree chase, but he knew his happiness wouldn't—couldn't—last. It was just that she was starting to wear him down with her charm. But if she wore him down, then that, coupled with the constant physical attraction that he still felt and knew was never going away, was sure to lead him straight into wanting to call off the divorce. And should that happen, they would only end up right back where they'd been before, with the desires she had that he didn't feel he could fulfill, and his own worries that he could never make her happy.

He couldn't let her wear him down.

Together, they entered the church. Six kids were at the front, facing the filled pews, singing their hearts out—and one of them was Molly.

Transfixed by the scene, Jared stood rooted there for a moment. The little ragamuffin who had popped up in the store while he'd been questioning people that afternoon now had her dusty cheeks scrubbed to a blushing pink. Atop her head she wore an angel's silver halo, and between the halo and her cloud of tawny hair, he thought he was seeing something almost…angelic.

Shea followed Jared's gaze and recognized Molly from his previous description and from the visit the child had made to her office. She ventured a glance back at her husband. Her heart skipped a beat. Jared's face had softened and she saw the hint of tears forming in his eyes.

Then he blinked and resumed his normal guarded look. But Shea had seen enough to tell her that the man did have a heart where children were concerned. For their baby's sake, she would have to keep on trying to thaw it out permanently.

The singing ended, the parishioners clapped, and then everyone seemed to be standing and milling about at once, with some heading toward a side door.

"We need to find Molly," Jared said, taking Shea's hand and leading her toward the front. His heart was telling him there was nothing at all special about the child, but there was. He just didn't understand what it was.

Molly spotted him first. Leaving the side of a petite woman in her forties, she ran to him. "You came! I knew you would come—Santa told me! He loved the tree!" She threw her arms around his legs. "Thank you so much."

Jared threw a "get me out of this" look at Shea. Stifling a grin, she bent down and took one of Molly's hands in her own. "Remember me, Molly? You dropped by my office the other day at Denton's department store. I'm Shea Burroughs."

Molly let go of Jared, then Shea heard his grateful sigh and hid her smile. The poor man really did seem terrified of children.

Molly turned to her mother, who had joined them. "This is Mr. Burroughs, Mama. He gave Santa the tree."

"Then I second my daughter's thanks, sir," Lucy Millstone said softly. Although she looked happy, she seemed very tired as she smiled at Shea. "And you, too, Mrs. Burroughs. It was so nice of you to make a little girl's wish come true."

"Oh, it was all Jared's idea," Shea told her and then smiled down at Molly, who was looking at Jared as if he was Santa Claus. "But I'm curious," she added. "You said Santa loved the tree? He's seen it already? How, when he doesn't come until Christmas?"

"He's already been here, at the church," Molly said solemnly, nodding her head. "He came early for us, and he saw the tree at the party. He said, 'It's a grand old tree.'" She spoke Santa's words in a low voice, as if the sentence had really come from St. Nick.

Shea looked up at Molly's mother, who laughed. "My daughter means the Santa who came to the church party we had about half an hour ago, right before the pageant. The children all got a present." She lifted a tote bag to show Jared and Shea a brightly wrapped gift tucked inside. "And your tree was the star attraction."

"I don't understand," Jared said. "I thought the tree was for you and Molly in your house."

Lucy shook her head. "Oh, no. The tree was for Santa's party. I'll show you." Taking Molly's hand, then beckoning Shea and Jared to follow, she walked through what was left of the crowd toward a door, then down a small hall, before she finally turned right into a large community room.

And that's where Shea found her tree.

It was dressed up in ornaments that only children could have made: paper chains, colored cutouts of Santa and candy canes and bells, and shiny tinfoil stars. It had no twinkling lights, it had no perfect crystal ornaments like the ones she had to put on her tree at home—but it was a glorious tree. Its stunted branches had been filled in by a big picture of Santa on his sleigh waving and grinning, and, Shea swore as her eyes filled with tears, winking at her.

Jared's arm slipped around her waist, and he pulled her close to him. "Still want the tree back, princess?"

"How could I?" She brushed away the tears. "I wouldn't touch that tree for the world. It ended up exactly where it was supposed to." Gazing up at him, she smiled. "Even with flaws, it's a perfect Christmas tree, isn't it?"

He groaned, but then shot her a big grin. "Didn't I tell you that?"

"Maybe I should start listening to you more," she said, sharing a smile with him. It was certainly something to consider. With a start, she recalled something that Molly had said, which sidetracked her, and she hurried back to the door where the two were waiting.

"Mrs. Millstone, I think you said that someone played Santa here this evening?"

Molly tugged at the bottom of her coat to get her attention. "No, not *played* Santa. He *is* Santa Claus."

Reaching under Molly's halo, Lucy gently stroked her daughter's curls. "I tried to explain to Molly that Santa is very busy making toys right now, and the Santa we had is just a very nice helper, but she seems to really believe this is the one." She shrugged in a parental, "you know how kids are" way.

"I'd like to see if he could help out at the store. Would you know where I can find him?"

A cautious expression on her face, Lucy looked down at Molly, and over her head so the child couldn't see, she nodded toward a smaller adjacent room. "Could we talk in there a minute?"

"If Molly would stay with Mr. Burroughs," Shea said, smiling at the little girl.

"Sure. I'll tell him what Santa's been telling me all about Christmas," she offered.

Jared shot her an "I'll get you for this" look, and Shea grinned back. It would be good practice for later, she wanted to say, but she knew that might be pushing her luck.

When the two of them were far enough away from Molly, but she and Jared were still in sight, Lucy gazed earnestly at her. "I don't know if you'll want to hire the man, Mrs. Burroughs—or if you'll even find him. I mean, our minister has a gracious, giving heart, but you might worry about the responsibility. The man truly believes he's Santa Claus, and..." Her voice trailed off.

"Mrs. Millstone, you don't have to worry. Please just tell me," Shea said.

"He's living at the Quiet Brook Shelter. I think he's a transient."

Oh, dear, Shea thought. "Well, I guess that might be something to check out. But how does Molly know him?"

"We've been living there, too, ever since a bit after her dad died and we lost the house," Lucy admitted, blushing bright red. "Not for long, I hope, but..." Unable to continue, she shook her head. "No, I shouldn't kid myself. It might be for a while, considering the Christmas rush will soon be over and the store won't need as much help."

"We'll see what happens then. Try not to worry." Even as Shea said the words, her heart was sinking.

They didn't need the extra help now, she knew. Later...if the store failed and closed, all their employees would be scrambling for jobs. She had no idea how to help Lucy Millstone and the adorable Molly.

She said the same to Jared when they were alone again in the truck. "I hadn't realized that we had anyone in the store in such dire straits."

"Your father must have if he hired her on without needing the help. He tries to protect you too much, Shea."

"He always has." She leaned her head back against the seat and closed her eyes. That was another thing she'd loved about Jared. From the start, he'd treated her like the successful, intelligent grown-up that she was. In the eyes of the town and her father, she would always be "that little Denton girl."

"Then Quiet Brook isn't the perfect place you thought it was?" he asked solemnly.

"Of course it is, Jared," she told him. "I can say that because I'm going to find a way to get that Santa to help us, and you're going to find the Grinch that wants to spoil Christmas around here, and then we're going to hang our baby's first ornament on the other tree you picked out and make this season in Quiet Brook perfect."

"And after that, I'll be leaving town."

No, he wouldn't, Shea vowed, leaning her head back again and refusing to be discouraged. No, he would not.

Jared glanced over at Shea. He was tired, aching from smelling the sweetness of her perfume, having her close and recalling the memories of the time when they were happy together. He had no doubt at all that spending the next hour or two searching for a transient who swore he was Santa was a preposterous idea. On the other hand, if he didn't help her find a substitute Santa and she was desperate enough to keep the store going, she might come up with some stupid plan concerning him, like…

No, it was too horrible to contemplate.

Chapter Seven

"I feel like a fool," Jared complained as Shea tugged at the back of his way-too-large Santa suit. Even with the pillow they'd stuffed in the front, she couldn't seem to make the gathers under the belt hang right.

"You need more backside," she said, smoothing the material as well as she could.

"Funny, that was never a problem for you before," he teased, wiggling his eyebrows, his mouth twisted with humor.

"I'm glad you're finding this so funny, Santa." She surely didn't. Despite the fact that she wasn't really touching that much of the real Jared, just the velveteen cloth and his belt, she felt nervous fussing over him. But it was necessary. "Quit fidgeting, Jared, or we'll never get out there."

He stretched his shoulders under the red suit. "It's

not that easy being an icon. I feel like a turkey, wrapped up in red velvet and headed for the slaughter.''

"You're two-thirds right," she told him and pushed his arms down.

"I'm not a turkey?"

"You aren't headed for the slaughter."

He grinned at her, and she grinned back.

The two of them were in a storeroom at Denton's. Outside the door, Shea could hear the children talking in excitement. Santa was back.

But not the shelter's Santa. Last night, while searching, she and Jared had discovered that the man who Molly swore was Santa had disappeared as swiftly and mysteriously as he had arrived. He was gone, along with the page in the register at the shelter that held his signature, so they hadn't even been able to find out his name.

Which had left them with no Santa. After Shea had launched what was to be a long, pleading and cajoling argument in which she was going to resort to reminding Jared about Mack's precarious health, Jared had shocked her by suddenly agreeing to play Santa. Just like that. She was finding it hard to believe how so much good could be mixed up with so much bad on this, the strangest of all her Christmases.

Feeling a curl from Santa's fake mustache tickling his nose, Jared resisted the urge to raise his arm to move it, because every time he did, Shea sighed and started her fussing with his suit all over again. As if her hands all over him wasn't troubling enough, he was feeling imprisoned by the massiveness of a heavy

velvet suit that meant so much to the children outside—and so little to him.

"I'm starting to sweat."

"It's nerves," Shea said.

"It's my worst nightmare."

"What is? Giving presents away?" she asked,
moving in front of him to make minor adjustments to
his beard and mustache.

"No, having to be jolly all day. I don't think I have
it in me."

She chuckled.

Even as he'd said it, Jared knew it wasn't the truth.
His true worst nightmare was to have her touching
him all over and being unable to touch her back, because his hands were tied down exactly as they were
right then—only in this case, by the weight of rep-
resenting a Christmas legend. And with Shea in her
white wig, granny glasses and a Mrs. Claus outfit,
looking close to the real thing, he was unnerved. He'd
never felt this close to Christmas before.

"No kidding, Shea. I'm not going to be any good
at this. I have no idea how to relate to kids."

"I know." As she stepped back and studied him,
her evergreen eyes sad, he realized he had just reminded her about more than merely the situation at
hand.

"Hell, I didn't mean to upset—"

"I know you didn't."

Standing on tiptoe, she gave him a quick kiss on
his cheek, which only demonstrated to Jared how far
apart they now were. Had it been a year ago, he'd
never have settled for so little.

"It's going to be okay, Jared," Shea reassured him. "I'll be right there with you. Just act jolly and follow my lead. It's not as difficult as you might think, getting used to kids. Look how much Molly likes you."

"I gave her church a tree."

"You cared about her. That's all it took."

"For her, not for me."

By the time she got through to Jared, Shea thought with a sigh, the baby was going to be driving. So he couldn't note the discouragement she was certain had to be on her face, she turned and walked over to the door. She had to keep trying and hang on to her hopes for a Christmas miracle. It was all she could do.

"Remember, Shea," he said as she turned the knob, "I'm only doing this so I can watch out for the Grinch."

And then he would be gone. Shea could hear the unspoken warning in his words, but she wasn't about to acknowledge it aloud. He was trying to make her give up on him. Well, she couldn't do it. She just couldn't give up her dreams of a wonderful life for her baby after she had pushed aside her dreams of a perfect marriage.

Opening the door, she found a small crowd of eager children who were waiting to see Santa as "Jingle Bells" played merrily over the loudspeaker. Moving to stand where she could block the children from running up the ramp to swarm Santa, she swept her arm up to indicate Jared—Santa—who was coming out of hiding.

"Attention, children!" she warbled gaily in her best Mrs. Claus voice. "Santa has arrived!"

The children began clapping and cheering. She knew she had to settle them down and get them in order to start visiting Santa, but first, she sneaked a look at Jared to make sure he hadn't walked straight off the Santa Station and out the door. He hadn't. As though he'd actually gained the extra pounds the suit represented, he was lumbering up to the seat of honor where he sat down on Santa's oversize chair with an "oomph."

Catching his eye, she mouthed to him, "Ho, ho, ho—Merry Christmas."

He stared at her blankly.

Resisting an overwhelming urge to throw her hands up in the air in exasperation, she faced the children.

"Merry Christmas!" she said, remembering to use the appropriate voice. "I know you've been waiting. Santa's eager to see you—" There was a loud "harrumph" behind her as Jared cleared his throat, which she chose to ignore. "And he has a present for each of you, so let's get started." She let the first little girl in line, the daughter of a friend of hers from school, pass her. As Lauren walked up the ramp to Santa, Shea smiled at the rest of the crowd. "Now who wants to sing along with the music on the speakers?"

Watching Shea work her magic with the kids, Jared knew he could never be that good with them. And then he looked down. Little Lauren was gazing at him as if he were a king. The bottom dropped out of his stomach. He didn't know what to say to her at first, but then Shea's tutorial kicked in.

"Uh, what can Santa do for you, little girl?" he

said, repeating exactly what Shea had told him to say—only it didn't sound quite the same, somehow.

"I have to go to the bathroom," she said. Then her lower lip went into a huge pout and her eyes misted with tears. "But I don't want to miss my turn!"

Bathroom. Hurriedly, he rose, took her hand and led her down the "leaving Santa" path to her mother, who hurried over from the sidelines where she'd been waiting. "Little girl's room," he told her, then trudged back up the path.

The next child, already waiting, was a towheaded boy who looked about eight and who stared at him suspiciously. Eight. He could almost remember eight, which gave him an idea of what to say.

"You don't want to sit on my lap, right?"

The boy continued to stare.

"Well, what can Santa bring you?" he asked, rewording Shea's message a little and wishing the kid would stop staring at him like he had hives or something. But then again, his neck was starting to itch, so maybe he did.

"Where's my present?"

His present? Jared looked down at the floor beside him. His Santa sack was in the workroom. He'd forgotten about it. Shea was going to have a fit and work him over. The one thing she probably wouldn't do, though, was fire him.

Shoot.

"I'll get it." Rising, he went into the workroom, where he found the sack and checked out its contents in case the Grinch had gotten there first. He found a bunch of Christmas coloring books and tiny crayons. Great. All set.

Rejoining the child, who had not given up his spot, Jared maneuvered his fake bulk into the chair and pulled out the giveaways. The boy's frown went deeper, and he shook his head. "I want candy."

Just jolly. "Candy will rot your teeth, kid."

Now the boy was scowling, and Jared was growing distinctly more uncomfortable. Shea was going to kill him.

"I'll bring you candy at Christmas," he promised. Then he remembered Shea's cardinal rule—don't promise them anything. Well, heck, surely the kid was going to get candy anyway.

The boy took the crayons and coloring book without a thank you, shook his head in disgust and walked away.

"Well, Merry Christmas to you, too," Jared said aloud, just as the music stopped.

Shea whipped around and looked down at the pint size bundle of trouble as he said in a voice loud enough for the store to hear, "That Santa's pitiful!"

Jared shut his eyes. Kids simply didn't relate to him. He was a washout as a Santa—just as he'd be a washout as a dad. So why was he sitting there, pretending to be something he was not?

The scent of soft ginger and a gentle movement next to him told him why. Shea. He would do anything for Shea that he possibly could—but his best would never be good enough.

"Jared."

He opened his eyes. Shea was inches from him,

leaning down, her soft cheek close enough to kiss. It took everything he had not to.

"Jared, please try a little harder," she whispered. "We consider even the children to be our customers." She smiled at him. "And you know the customer is always right."

"That kid was too young to buy anything," he protested.

"You really don't know anything about today's kids, do you? He's eight. I'll bet he's loaded."

"Yeah, maybe. But he didn't even say thank-you." He shifted uncomfortably. Shea's nearness was making him want to bolt. "I think that kid might be the Grinch. I should ditch the suit and keep an eye on him while he shops. Make sure he doesn't shoot out the lights on your display trees with a BB gun."

Shea laughed. "I can see I'd better stay close and help you get through this torture." She straightened up, but her ginger scent lingered in the air around him. He shouldn't have noticed, but he did.

"You mean you'll suffer with me?" He wasn't sure he was referring just to the role of Santa, either.

"Honestly, Jared, it's not that bad. Watch."

Turning before he could argue, she beckoned the next child up with a flick of her finger, like a fairy godmother working her magic. And suddenly, Jared was glad she was near and he wasn't alone. Having her by his side felt so very right.

By the time the four hours were up, Shea decided Jared might just have the hang of it. It only took a few of his ho, ho, hos and the air of excitement she tried her darnedest to create with smiles and lots of encouragement, and the kids were laughing and having fun with the new Santa.

When Molly showed up, Jared went all the way and even insisted he truly was Santa until the little girl was giggling with delight. Then Molly took out her list of Christmas wishes to show him.

"If you're really Santa," she said, "you'll be able to read this."

Jared looked down at the list. In one corner was a Christmas tree with presents underneath in every color from neon purple to orange, and across the top was a childlike scrawl that sort of resembled writing, but not quite.

"Hmm," he said, "let's see. 'Dear Santa.'"

She nodded. "But that's how everybody starts their letters."

He stared down at the rest and was forced to improvise. "Bike?" he guessed.

She shook her head and took the list from him. "Nope. You're Mr. Burroughs all right. But that's okay, because I like you."

Jared felt a warm glow grow inside him, a sensation totally alien to him.

Turning, Molly tugged on Shea's sleeve. "I have something to tell you both," she said.

Shea leaned down close to her so she could hear Molly's soft voice over the store music.

"The real Santa had to leave Quiet Brook," Molly said, looking from Shea to Jared. "But he said he would come back one more time."

"For Christmas, right?" Shea asked, casting Jared

a long, "what do you make of this" look. Jared just shrugged.

Molly did the same. "I don't know."

"Well, I'm positive he meant for Christmas." Shea waited as Jared reached into his bag and gave Molly her goodies. "Make sure you come back tomorrow, Molly. Santa's going to give out stockings to each of the kids."

Molly gave her a big grin. "Okay. I'll keep it secret that the real Santa's gone and Mr. Burroughs's just here for a little while."

As Shea watched Molly lean forward and give Jared a quick kiss on his cheek on top of the white whiskers, the child's words tugged at her heart. Jared would be here only for a little while. All the fun they'd had that day, all the laughter, would soon be gone. It was a disheartening thought.

Seconds later, Molly scampered from the Santa Station and disappeared into the store. As Jared stared after her, Shea watched him. His deep blue eyes were smiling. It was a miracle—although not quite the one she wanted.

"That's a cute kid," he said. "I'll bet her father adored her before he died."

That he would even think about such a thing thrilled Shea. "I'll bet he does now, too, from up in heaven."

"Kid like that should have a father watching out for her—down here."

Jared was worried about Molly. Shea had thrown him into the pool—was he beginning to swim, if only enough to keep his head above water? Was he actually loosening up?

Shea had to keep trying, find more things to make him experience the happiness he'd obviously felt for a brief time with Molly. But she couldn't push. He'd see through that.

Leaving Jared's side now that the last child was gone—until the evening crowd of shoppers anyway—she flipped over the Open sign to Closed and latched the gate at the foot of the path. A few seconds later, Jared's almost empty Santa sack in her hand, she joined him on the short walk to the storeroom.

"You made it," she said cheerfully. "And you're still in one piece."

Jared thought back to one child who had swung her little leg, hitting her heel into his shin over and over, and to another little child whose elbow had caught him right in the nose as he climbed down from Santa's lap. "I'm dented, though."

"Like you mentioned before, Jared," she said cheerfully, "a few flaws build character."

He groaned. "I should have known you wouldn't offer to kiss the dents and make them better."

"No way." She shut the storeroom door behind them. "I kind of like the way you're shaping up." Turning, she was startled to find him in her way.

Inches from her, Jared knew he should move, but he couldn't. She was so close, and he desperately wanted to kiss her.

"You like the way I'm shaping up?" he asked, his voice husky. He had to call a halt before he forgot himself and tried to seduce Mama Christmas, promising her something he couldn't give her. Managing a weak grin, he patted his pillowed belly. "You like the well-fed look?"

Feeling the tension melt away, she grinned back. "I'd better. My turn's coming in the next six months."

Because she was going to have a baby, all she'd ever wanted, Shea was wearing her heart in her eyes. It made Jared realize whether round with child or slim as she was at the moment, she would always be beautiful.

He had to stop thinking like this. Moving toward the table where he'd left his clothes, he unbuckled his wide black belt and started unbuttoning the jacket of the Santa suit. While he did that, Shea began scanning the shelves and peering into and behind a stack of empty boxes in one corner.

"What are you looking for?" he asked, setting the pillow aside and allowing himself a deep sigh of relief. "Signs of sabotage?"

"I'm just checking. You never know. I expect the Grinch to make some attempt to drive you away from Denton's very soon."

"Maybe. Or maybe he's had his fun or finally realized you won't give up."

"Maybe," Shea echoed, not believing it for one minute.

Returning to her search, she tried to forget that he'd almost kissed her a couple of minutes before and that she'd wanted him to. That she had wanted him back as her husband.

She couldn't think like that. Could she? Was she

willing to go back into a marriage with a man who had no understanding of the things that made her so happy, even if he accepted their baby?

She didn't know if she could chance the heartbreak all over again if it didn't work out. And she wouldn't do that to her baby, either. She wanted a perfect life for them here in Quiet Brook, with all the trimmings. Jared was so far removed from that point.

She glanced at him, his dark wavy hair, his quiet, thoughtful eyes. He was a brave, wonderful man. He had treated her as an equal, and he had loved her the best way he knew how, but it just hadn't been enough. He held too much back and he'd let her go without a fight. He didn't expect to change, or even want to, so how could she even consider a future with him again?

She had to remain strong. She had to show Jared what she knew about the joys of Christmas, her small-town life and children and hope it would be enough to help him find some happiness in his own life.

Pushing the painful question of their relationship to the back of her mind, Shea walked over to the three boxes of stockings filled with little plastic toys they were giving out the next day. Everything looked fine, which meant the Grinch was still out there, getting ready to strike—and that meant that Jared needed to stick around another day.

One more day to try to reach him.

"I'm really proud of you, you know," she said, turning toward him, smiling, wanting him to know how happy she was that he was helping the store to succeed. But then she saw he was half dressed, pulling on his flannel shirt over bare arms and a solid torso, and her heart did a double flip. He'd obviously been working out. He'd always been in good shape, but this was...was... "The new and improved Jared," she managed to say lightly, hoping her desire for him wasn't written all over her face. How could she want a man so desperately who was all wrong for her?

"Impressed?" he asked, buttoning his shirt and giving her a crooked grin. "I've had a lot of spare time on my hands. I've used it to work out."

Impressed wasn't the word for what she was feeling, but she couldn't tell him that. Reminding herself it was wrong to only want him for his body, she leaned back against the table and wondered what had happened to her common sense. She was ready to throw her happiness away, go back to him and beg him to take her.

Right now.

On the worktable.

She shook her head to clear it. He was staring at her, and she blinked and smiled.

"Are you staying to watch me switch to my jeans?" he asked, pointing to his floppy red Santa pants.

"No!" Her face heating, she rushed toward the door and slid out into the magical world of Christmas at Denton's. She'd change at home, she decided, safely away from Jared.

As she headed for the escalators to tell her dad she was leaving for the day, humming along with the Christmas carol and waving at customers who grinned at her in her Mrs. Claus outfit, she realized she was happy.

Happy. For now. Because of Jared. If only she could pull off a miracle...

But she knew she couldn't. He needed to learn not to be afraid to open himself up and care about people and the little things in life that meant so much to others. It would take years for her to work that kind of total change in him—if she ever could. And she couldn't spend years of her life, only to end up unhappy if she failed at helping him.

She couldn't chance getting that involved. She was too afraid that he would change her and make her close down her emotions just to be able to cope, and she didn't want to be like that, not caring about the wonderful things in life. She didn't want him to change her.

The trouble was, much as she was afraid she'd be unhappy with him, she was beginning to wonder if she was going to be just as unhappy without him.

The next day went more smoothly; Jared even felt like he was getting the hang of things. While he couldn't say he was exactly enjoying himself, playing Santa wasn't the torture it had been the day before—unless you counted the fact that he was, at times, once again inches from Shea.

He ached deep inside with the awareness that every second they spent together brought him one minute closer to his returning to Topeka and the countdown to their divorce. And the divorce was inevitable. He couldn't ask Shea to be anyone but who she was, with her constant search for happiness and perfection in a world that had anything but. Still, he thought he could live with her being that way as long as she would accept him exactly the way he was in return. But she couldn't seem to. He really couldn't blame her. After all, he didn't want her to live her life being miserable.

And then there was the matter of their child. He would have to change entirely to be a good father. Yet he knew he couldn't change the way he was. Much as he would like to be, he'd never be like Mack with his love of his hometown and its traditions and his ability to relate and reach out to people. It was clear that that was what Shea wanted for their child so it would have a life like the one she'd had. Shoot, if truth be told, that would be his wish for their baby, too. A daddy who could show his love.

That's why he knew the divorce had to go through.

Shea was going to make a wonderful mother, Jared mused, as he watched her handle the kids in line. She leaned over the next child, a toddler who looked like he didn't particularly want to meet Santa but had a mother who insisted. The way Shea quieted the child with a gentle touch on his cheek and soft words Jared couldn't hear made him yearn for what he had missed in his own childhood, growing up with a father who didn't know the word hug. It was this part of Shea that made him wish he could be what she wanted and needed for herself.

The boy finally stopped crying, and Jared felt relieved. Only his relief was extremely short-lived as the mother, who looked just out of her teenage years and rather frazzled, brought the toddler up to him.

"I was hoping to get a picture of Bryan with Santa for his great-grandmother," the young woman said, setting the child on his lap. Her brown eyes were serious. "She's really old, in a nursing home, and children are the only thing that make her smile."

Jared looked from the mother to little Bryan, who pouted and scrunched his eyes. "I'll do my best," he promised.

Looking doubtful, the mother headed down the ramp, raised her camera and waited.

Jared leaned down close to the toddler's ear and said in a cooing, sympathetic voice like the one he'd heard Shea use on a little one earlier, "So, tell me, kid, how do you like growing up in Quiet Brook? Is it nice here? You've got to tell me, because I know a little baby who's going to be around here soon and I want him to be happy."

The toddler forgot to pout and looked up at Jared with interest, and that's when Jared felt the lump in his throat.

"Atta boy," he said. "Smile for your great-grandma so she'll smile back when she sees your picture." Little Bryan let out a couple of syllables and smiled, and his mother snapped a picture. Bryan put a tiny hand on his beard and pulled. Jared laughed. "Yeah, kid, there is a real man under all that fluff."

Bryan let out a gurgle of sheer happiness that chipped away an inch or two of the ice around Jared's heart, and he felt an overwhelming need to connect with Shea. Looking up, he found her in the crowd. She was already watching him, a smile on her face.

As the little boy toddled down the ramp with his mother, Shea approached him, and he rose.

"What did you say to that child?" Shea asked softly. Once again, just like the day before, her spicy perfume filled the air, making him think of warm cookies and motherhood and love. "Jared?" she prompted.

He met Shea's eyes. Little Bryan. Oh, yeah. "I told him that Santa was going to bring him goodies."

One dark eyebrow lifted. "I tried that. It didn't work."

"Well, you weren't Santa," he said, grinning.

She laughed suddenly, merrily, her laughter harmonizing with the jolly Christmas carol that was floating down around them. Then, just as unexpectedly, she stood on tiptoe and kissed him, her lips covering his with warmth and sweetness. And right before she pulled away, she added in a soft, breathy whisper, "Merry Christmas, Jared."

Not wanting to lose the moment, he reached around and pulled her to his pillowed girth, kissing her back, losing his mind in that kiss, until applause exploded around them.

Breaking away, he grinned sheepishly at the mothers and the older folks seated at the refreshment area who were clapping. "I can't say I've ever felt this appreciated—and needed—before," he told her.

"Not even by me?" Shea asked lightly, but there was a trace of seriousness edging her voice.

He shook his head. "Maybe at first, for a little while. But after that, you stopped showing me."

"I did?" she asked, looking so very puzzled Jared

didn't know what to think. But he did know what he
wanted to do. Catching her to him again, he finished
what he'd started, kissing her as if they'd been married as long as the real Santa and his wife, kissing her
as if they were never going to part.

Finally, the clapping quieted, and remembering
where they were, Jared reluctantly let her go. He expected her to ask if he'd lost his mind, but she just
gazed at him, looking as dazed as he felt.

"We need to talk, I think," he said.

She nodded solemnly, backing away as a trio of
mothers ventured forth.

"And here we were thinking that no one stayed
married anymore," one of the women said, giggling.

At that innocent comment, Shea's heart clenched
and her eyes heated with tears. It, along with Jared's
remark that she'd stopped showing she needed him
and his hot kiss that made her think she was crazy
for leaving him, made her feel unsure what she really
wanted anymore.

Taking a step backward, she left Jared with the
women and turned to go to the storeroom to wait by
herself for him to finish talking to the happy moms.
She could hear them buzzing around him, which she
loved. He needed to know the good he was doing.

"You were a miracle worker with little Bryan,"
one woman was saying. "That child cried all through
the church service last Sunday. How did you do it?"

"I'm Santa Claus," Jared said. "And someone
very wise told me this is the season of miracles."

She'd told him that the same time as she'd told
him she was carrying his child. He'd been listening

to her after all, Shea realized, her heart filling with joy. While she waited, she thought over the questions she wanted to ask Jared. He'd kissed her as if they had plenty of tomorrows. Were his feelings changing toward her? Why had he thought she didn't need him? Had she stopped showing him?

Did they have a chance?

She clearly had some self-examining to do. Could their breakup really have been partly her fault? Could she have forgotten to show Jared how much she loved him?

Filled with confusion and self-doubt, Shea opened the door to the storeroom, slipped inside almost soundlessly and shut out the world behind her. She needed to know...to talk to him...to figure it out—

"Tarnation!"

Still caught in tumultuous thoughts of Jared, Shea stared at a man with eyes just as shocked as hers. He was kneeling next to the two remaining cardboard boxes of stockings Santa was going to hand out to the children...and sabotaging them with lumps of coal from a pile near one booted foot.

Shocked, Shea only had time to mutter, "Why are you doing this?" before the Grinch rose to his feet and tore off through another door leading directly into a side hall and then outside Denton's, leaving her only with questions rather than answers—and a more immediate problem.

Now that she'd discovered the identity of the Grinch, how on earth was she going to keep Jared in Quiet Brook?

Chapter Eight

Every instinct told Shea she had to follow Mr. Griswold, the Grinch, not only to buy time to consider what to do now about keeping Jared in Quiet Brook, but also to find out why on earth the elderly man had been up to such mean-spirited tricks. Thanking her lucky stars that she'd kept her leggings, socks and long sweater on under the Mrs. Claus outfit for padding, Shea hurriedly stripped off the costume, changed shoes and grabbed her jacket. But she was seconds too slow. Just as she was about to slip out the same door Mr. Griswold had gone through, Jared joined her.

They stood there staring at each other, Jared on his way in and Shea on her way out, her hand on the doorknob, the door partially opened.

"This isn't how it looks," she said. "I really want to talk to you, Jared—only not right now. Something's come up I have to attend to."

"Okay," he said slowly. He took on the same guarded look he'd worn so often during their marriage, and she knew this time, it really was her fault. This time, he'd been reaching out to her, but she was too afraid to tell him the truth, that he no longer had a reason to stay.

What if he agreed?

"We're going to talk as soon as I get back, Jared," she promised. "I really want to." And then, convinced she was doing the best thing for them, she hurried out.

Now that, Jared thought, staring at the empty place where Shea had just been, was the last thing he'd expected when he'd walked through the storeroom door. She didn't really think he was just going to sit around and wait for her to return and tell him what that was all about, now did she? Surely she knew him better than that—didn't she?

A quick scan of the room confirmed what he had half guessed—that the only thing more important to her, at the moment anyway, than cementing their relationship for the baby's sake, was catching the store's Grinch. It was clearly evident that someone had been there wreaking havoc. Coal spilled out of an overturned burlap sack, and in its midst was a handful of hard candies in shiny green, red and white wrappers that had originally been in one of the Christmas stockings. She must have caught the practical joker in the act when she'd left him earlier.

Knowing that with his fake beard and his street clothes on underneath his heavy Santa suit, he was padded well enough against the cold that he didn't feel anyway, Jared followed her through the door. In the hall, he saw the fire-exit door shutting behind her, so he turned and headed toward it. After that, it was a relatively easy matter to trail her, keeping enough distance behind so she wouldn't particularly notice him unless she turned fully around.

"Merry Christmas, Santa!" a woman called out cheerfully as she passed him near the very next storefront. "Good to see you out here!"

"Merry Christmas to you, too," he replied. At least that part was becoming easier after all the practice with the kids. He wanted to walk faster so the rest of the pedestrians could tell he was a Santa on a mission and leave him alone, but if he went too fast, he would catch up to Shea. So he continued to stroll, keeping Shea in his sights.

And as he walked, waving with his white gloved hand at the people who smiled at seeing a sidewalk Santa roving Main Street again, he started noticing the details of the upcoming holiday he hadn't paid attention to in a long, long time. Christmas lights, strung high in the air, stretched across the street every twenty feet or so in the patterns of a reindeer, a Christmas tree and then a green-wrapped box with a red bow. Since the sky was already growing dim with approaching evening, they were lit, adding to the holiday sparkle. In one storefront window to his left were presents on display, their wrapping paper sporting cartoon characters dressed up like Santa. At the corner store, a wooden toy soldier towered over Jared. And someone, somewhere, had turned on a speaker, and a choir was singing a Christmas hymn.

But suddenly noticing all these things didn't change the simple fact that he wasn't feeling whatever the hell it was he was supposed to be feeling. Spirit? Joy? All warm inside? All he felt was a kind of emptiness, a Santa just going through the motions.

No, more precisely, he felt like a man just going through the motions of living. He no longer had the wife he'd loved as best he could; he wouldn't be a fit father for his son—or daughter—and he was going to spend the rest of his life alone.

Just like his Grinch of a father.

After crossing the street, Jared stopped short near the courthouse, a two-story limestone building with a courtyard in the front. In the midst of the courtyard was a huge Christmas tree, and it was there, a few feet down on the walkway that curved around the far side of the tree, where he spotted Shea with Mack's elderly neighbor from across the street. Gris something. Griswold, that was it.

Rounding the reverse side of the tree, he moved in closer until he could hear them, then stood there like a Santa mannequin posing in a Christmas scene. He ought to feel guilty for eavesdropping on Shea, he supposed, but he didn't. Now that he was thinking about it, in fact, he wasn't too happy with Shea for not telling him that the Grinch had been discovered before she headed out the door.

Their voices lowered, and to hear them he moved into the branches a bit more.

"Even if you don't care about Dad and our store," he could hear Shea saying, "don't you understand how you almost ruined Christmas for all the kids?"

Keeping a wary eye out for anyone leaving the courthouse, Jared moved a branch to get a better glimpse of Shea. Her hand was on the elderly man's forearm. To keep him from running away? He didn't know much about Mack's neighbor, except what Shea had told him, but he didn't think the guy was dangerous. Still, it seemed as if he should be on the alert, but for what, he didn't know.

"I never worried about the kids," Griswold said, sounding winded from the chase. "I only knew everybody in town was having too much fun. In the store. Outside. Everybody's happy but me."

"It hasn't particularly been my year, either, Mr. Griswold," Shea said with a sigh that cut through Jared. "But that's what Christmas is for. To renew your spirit, remind you how good the world is."

Griswold muttered under his breath.

"Was that *humbug* you just said?" Shea asked. Jared could hear the hint of laughter in her voice, but a casual bystander who didn't know her as well would think she was scolding. "Shame on you, Mr. Griswold. This is serious. Do you know how much Dad has been worrying? Your shenanigans have been hurting business in the store and causing him stress. If we have a bad Christmas after the slowdown and renovations earlier this year, we could lose Denton's. I don't even want to think about what that might do to him. He has heart problems, you know."

There was a pause. "I didn't know that." Another pause. "Things aren't that good at the store?"

"No, they aren't," Shea said firmly. "The children all wanted to see Santa, so their parents have been driving them to the mall and shopping there instead of with us. Fortunately, with Jared playing Santa yesterday, sales picked up some in the evening, and I'm looking forward to an even better report today.''

He hadn't wanted to do it and didn't want to admit it, Jared thought, but he could see that, just maybe, his playing Santa had been a good thing.

''Why did you do this, Mr. Griswold?'' Shea was asking. ''Are you angry with Dad about something?''

Shaking his head slowly, Mr. Griswold looked as guilty as a small child caught tracking mud on a clean kitchen floor. He gazed down at his feet as though he wished they would carry him away. ''My wife left me, took the grandson.''

Jared swallowed. There was a little too much similarity between him and Griswold for his liking.

''I'm so sorry things turned out that way,'' Shea said softly.

''Yeah, well,'' Griswold said, shuffling his feet, ''said she ain't coming back till after Christmas is over. Said I was too grumpy. Said I didn't enjoy the holiday enough and she was danged if she was going to spend another Christmas with me and my moods. I told her I wasn't going to change one dang thing about myself because she's lived with me for forty years this way and oughta be used to it. That's when she left.''

''Christmas is a very magical time, Mr. Griswold. Maybe she just wanted to make sure she got some of that magic for herself and your grandson this year, and you were making it too hard. When you didn't help her to have a merry Christmas season, maybe she thought you didn't care if she was happy or not.''

Shea could have been speaking directly to him, Jared reflected. But the very idea was ridiculous. Not care? She was the reason he came home every night. She had to have realized that even when he'd reached the conclusion that he never wanted children.

Yeah, sure, just like she knew how you felt about being needed for yourself, Burroughs.

"You mean," Griswold was saying, "that each time I complained and she couldn't make things okay, she felt bad?''

"That's what I think," Shea replied. "I'll bet mostly she wanted you to be happy, and when you weren't, or when you didn't talk to her, especially at this time of the year, it made her sad that you couldn't see the fun in the season—or in life. And believe me, Mr. Griswold, when you're basically a happy, optimistic type like Mrs. Griswold, it's hard to be around somebody sad all the time.''

What Shea was saying told Jared a lot about her perspective on their breakup. Since he'd never wanted to argue with Shea, he'd just walked away when she said something that he disagreed with. It had been his father's way of coping with life. Silence. He hadn't always been like that. He remembered wishing he had someone to talk to when he was a kid. But he had turned into his father nevertheless. And that wasn't good.

Unless he figured some way out of it, he was going to end up just like his father and Griswold. Old, alone and unhappy. Hell, he didn't want that for himself.

The only trouble was, he didn't know how to stop what seemed like his destiny. The conversation was resuming, so he forced himself to listen, feeling eerily as if he'd met up with the Ghost of Christmas Future.

"So it was after Mrs. Griswold left you that you started hanging around the store all the time, and everything and everyone was so cheerful you couldn't stand it? That's when you started—" she paused "—*fixing* things?"

Griswold nodded. "Then the store got sort of deserted, and I could almost pretend there wasn't going to be a Christmas."

"There almost wasn't one," Shea assured him, "until Jared came and saved the day."

"Yeah. And I got caught." The old man's head bowed, then he gave her a worried look. "So what're you gonna do, Shea? Call Ed?"

Ed was the town's police chief, Jared remembered.

"You're an old family friend," Shea said gently. "As long as you stop the meanness, I won't turn you in."

Somehow that didn't surprise Jared. His wife's enormous heart was one of the reasons he'd fallen in love with her.

"You mean you're letting me get away with this?" Griswold asked.

"Of course not. You have to tell my father that you were the one doing all the mean-spirited practical jokes."

"Won't that be kind of stressful for him?" Griswold asked, sounding truly concerned. "I'm not going to do anything else. I was kind of thinking I just wouldn't come back in the store. I figured giving up my favorite place to sit in the afternoons and staying home instead would be punishment enough.''

"Your being forced to stay home all day would only be punishment for Mrs. Griswold when she comes back, I'm afraid," Shea said, chuckling.

Somewhere deep inside him, Jared chuckled right along with her. God, he loved her. She was warmth and happiness—everything he needed.

He was everything she didn't.

He wanted to stay around her, try to become the person she wanted, see if it would work. He wanted to, but he was afraid that she was seeing him through all too idealistic eyes, thinking that he could even be a good father.

Sounding somewhat reluctant, Griswold agreed to her terms.

"And there's one other thing I want you to do," Shea said. "Promise to come to dinner at our house on Christmas Eve."

Griswold was quiet for a few seconds, and Jared thought the man sounded kind of choked up when he finally spoke.

"I'll be there, missy, if you'll let me walk you back to the store. It's after dark, and you shouldn't be out by yourself."

Shea's laughter rang through the night air. "You sure letting the town's Grinch escort me anywhere is safe?"

"You betcha!" Griswold said. "You know, if I live through telling your father I've been a fool, I'm gonna call my wife and see if I can apologize to her.

And if I survive doing that, this might not turn out to be such a bad Christmas after all.''

This time, Shea didn't laugh in agreement, which left Jared feeling like maybe, just maybe, he ought to do something about saving Shea's Christmas.

But what?

Back at the store, her father surprised Shea by taking the news Caleb Griswold gave him remarkably well. He even said he understood and was just glad it was over. The two men shook hands, with Griswold vowing to reform, call his wife, apologize and beg her to come home. Everything went smoothly.

After Griswold left, closing the office door behind him, Shea voiced her request to keep the news that the Grinch had been caught a secret. It was then that Mack actually started going red in the face.

"Maybe you'd better sit down, Dad."

"Of course we're going to tell everyone the Grinch has been caught." Mack hit the desktop with his fist for emphasis. "We just aren't going to say who it was."

"Maybe I'd better sit down." Shea sank into the chair across from him, feeling the day's events catching up with her. Either she was still chilled from standing outside so long with the Grinch, or she was nervous about her father saying no. She wasn't sure, but she couldn't seem to get warm.

Briefly, she thought about Jared's arms around her. That brought a blush to her cheeks, but unfortunately, if she couldn't get her father to agree to her request, she doubted if she was going to have much of a chance to get that close to Jared again. He'd be gone.

Seeming to sense something was wrong, her father got up and rounded his desk. He stopped abruptly, looking unsure of himself. "I'm sorry, Shea. I didn't mean to startle you. Are you all right?" His frown deepened. "Should I find Jared?"

"No," she said hurriedly, not quite ready to face him yet. "That's all right. I'll go find him later. I'm just tired." Tired and worried. She was so close to changing Jared's attitude about children. She could see it in the way his dark blue eyes became more and more easy whenever a child approached him. Darn it all, she wanted that chance to change him.

For the baby's sake.

Mack sat on the edge of his desk and crossed his arms over his chest. "Okay, so tell me why you don't want the town to know Denton's is Grinch free."

"I don't want Jared to go," she said softly. "I want him to stay on as Santa. I need a little more time with him, and if he finds out he's not needed, he'll leave."

Her father gave her a long look. "The divorce is final in less than a week, baby. Are you thinking to stop it?"

Was she? Was that even possible? Jared would have to be a different man for her to call off the divorce. She didn't want to spend the next forty years the way Mrs. Griswold apparently had, having a man in her life who never understood her or fitted into the happy life she wanted. Shea knew she needed Jared to care about traditions and community and family and believe they were all as important as she believed they were.

But that could take a lifetime and still not happen.

Sadness threatening to overwhelm her, Shea shook her head. "In the long run, I guess I'm just trying to make this Christmas perfect for Jared, you and me. As perfect as it can be, anyway."

Mack took so long to answer that Shea was certain he was going to refuse her request. Then he sighed. "I'm not sure keeping a secret from him is the best way to handle it, but I'm going to bow to your judgment this time. As long as Jared agrees to play Santa and the parents keep coming, you don't have to tell anyone you caught the Grinch." Leaning over, he patted her arm. "But, dear heart, as for you and Jared, maybe you'd better quit looking for what you already have."

"What does that mean?"

"You're a smart girl. You'll figure it out—and I can only hope you do before it's too late." He got up and walked toward the coat rack to pull on his coat, but then he paused by the door. "By the way, that little Molly girl stopped in to see me. Cute little thing."

"Yes, she is."

"Fanciful, too. Says she's become Santa's elf now and she's helping him out until he gets back into town."

The image made Shea smile. The child was adorable. "If she's an elf and that Santa of hers is as real as she claims, maybe I should get her to throw a little Christmas magic my way."

"Yes, well…" Mack cleared his throat and started blushing. "I was thinking more along the line of my throwing a little her way. What would you say if I rented the garage apartment to her and her mother?"

"I'd say that's a wonderful idea!" Rising, she joined him at the door, beaming at him and temporarily forgetting her troubled relationship. "But the apartment's so small, you couldn't possibly rent that thing for more than a hundred and a half a month, you know."

"Yeah, I kind of figured I wasn't going to make a killing off it." He grinned back.

"So if they're going to be our neighbors, you know that means we'll probably have to have them over for Christmas Eve dinner. Sure you can stand the crowd and the noise? If Jared stays, that'll be four extra."

"Five if you count my impending grandchild." His thick brows rose in question. "So can I take it you approve of my idea?"

"A child in the house on Christmas Eve?" Her heart quickened with bittersweet joy. Between Griswold and the Millstones, their home would be bustling this season. All she had to do now was bake a lot of cookies—and insure that Jared was a part of it, too. "Of course I approve."

He beamed back at her and went off to play his own version of Santa Claus to the Millstones.

As she headed downstairs to look for Jared, she considered what she was about to do. It wasn't right, lying to Jared. But he was so close to being able to give his heart to their baby-to-be and wanting to be a great father that she was sure she could find some way to push him over the edge—if she just had a little more time. So really, what choice did she have?

Her nerves getting more tender with every second, Shea began to hum along with the store's Christmas carols as she walked around looking for Jared. When she finally found him in a booth at the rear of the snack area near the Santa Station, her eyes took in the sight of him in his jeans, midnight blue flannel shirt and tousled dark brown hair. Then her heart hustled up a different song that had more to do with desire than Christmas. She slid into the booth opposite him, trying to shush her heart.

His eyes met hers questioningly, and her throat closed in an uncharacteristic surge of pure panic. She didn't want to lie to him. But she had to. For the baby's sake.

And maybe even for her own.

"I saw the coal in the storeroom and figured that that was what had you so preoccupied," he said when she didn't speak. "Did you see who it was?"

"I missed the Grinch by seconds," she said, reaching down and picking up his untouched glass of water to take a sip. When she put it back down on the table, her fingers remained around the bottom in a tight, tense grip. "I thought maybe I could catch up with whoever it was if I didn't stop to explain, but even though I searched around for a while, I didn't find out who it was."

He nodded. "I know. After I changed out of the Santa suit, I checked the alley. He could have disappeared anywhere, so I came back in here."

Flooded with relief that he seemed to have swallowed her story, Shea relaxed her fingers. "I wasn't kidding when I said it before, Jared. We need you more than ever here. We want you to stay.''

''We?'' he asked quietly.

''I do.'' She met his eyes and was startlingly aware of just how calm they were. Controlled. She couldn't decide if that was good—or bad. ''You actually talked to me before, Jared, about how you felt when we were together.''

Her hands shook a little, and she laid them one over the other on the table in front of her. She was about to head into the same territory that had led to her walking out before, and kiss or no kiss, it was scary.

''You said I stopped showing you I needed you.'' She took a deep breath. ''I hadn't realized that. I got so involved with my ideas of making everything so wonderful for our future that I forgot, I guess, just to live for the day sometimes and that it would be your future, too.'' She glanced down at her hand, at the finger that used to hold his ring. ''I forgot to make sure you knew that I loved you, no matter what. I'm so sorry for that.''

Jared reached across the table and put his large, warm hand over hers. Her gaze lifted to meet his eyes, and as she looked at him, her heart began beating thunderously in her chest. Was he going to say that he wanted them to try again?

And if he did, would she accept? Almost every part of her wanted to fall into his arms and make the hurt of the past months go away, but there was still a tiny voice within her—the voice of reason?—that wouldn't let her forget that she could never live with the remote man he'd turned into, the man who didn't seem to care about all the things that were so important to her....

Like their baby.

But he wasn't saying a thing.

"Say you'll stay, Jared," she asked. "Please? I promise you won't regret it." And he wouldn't. She'd learned her lesson. She was going to try harder to use love to make his life better—both for him and their baby.

"You mean stay long enough to catch the Grinch, right?" he asked in return, his thumb moving over her fingers, his touch fueling the fire within her that had never totally burned out when they'd parted.

She was caught. If she asked him to stay just to work on their relationship and he refused, she would have blown her chance to keep him there. If he did agree, and she didn't get him to warm up, she'd end up hurting him in the end once more because she didn't want to raise the child in a family with a cold and distant father.

"Stay long enough to save Christmas for me," she whispered. That was as close as she could put it and still say the truth—but she knew Jared wouldn't be able to interpret that the way she meant it. He didn't know what was in her heart.

His thumb stopped its soothing movement, and his eyes searched hers as he considered her request. His answer came sooner than she expected.

"Okay, I'll stay. But Shea..." His hand tightened on hers. Not enough to hurt, but the pressure felt almost like a warning.

"Yes?" she asked, regaining some of her voice now that she knew she'd bought some time.

"I'm not promising a thing."

Chapter Nine

"This Christmas is getting better all the time," Shea said as she danced with Jared at a church Christmas party on Sunday afternoon. "You know the Griswolds across the street from Dad's house?"

"The old guy we saw in the store?" Jared tried to remain nonchalant, but inside, he tensed. Was she actually going to tell him she'd found the Grinch? Finally?

"That's right. Well, he'd been fighting with his wife, and she was spending Christmas elsewhere. He was pretty upset. But Dad told me earlier that Mr. Griswold convinced his wife he's a changed man, and she came home last night. So all the Griswolds will be joining us on Christmas Eve."

Jared waited, but Shea didn't add anything about having discovered that Griswold was the Grinch. Disappointed, he muttered, "That's nice," and pulled her close to him, not wanting to give her a chance to ask the obvious question—whether or not he'd still be in Quiet Brook on Friday.

She snuggled against him, and in turn he held her like there would be no tomorrow—which was the truth. He would be leaving before Shea got up the next morning.

It had been over two days since the Grinch had been found. Saturday, he'd played Santa and watched Shea for any signs to explain why she wanted to keep him in town so desperately that she would lie to him about being needed when he wasn't. But her lovely eyes had given away nothing.

Her cheek had been resting against his shoulder as they danced to a slow song. But she must have sensed the growing tension inside him, for she raised her eyes to his, her smile anxious.

"Did you like what Santa brought you this morning?"

"Yeah." He pulled her back to him and nuzzled his face against her sweet-smelling hair. He'd woken up that morning in Mack's guest room to find three wrapped presents on his bed, which turned out to be video games and collectible model cars. Toys. She was trying so hard to give him back the childhood Christmases he'd missed, and he appreciated the gesture.

Except he had felt none of the thrill he knew he should have felt at the surprise. When he caught the expression on his face in the mirror on the dresser after he'd found the presents, he'd realized it was one of indifference. He could never look like that in front of his kid on Christmas morning. If he stayed, he would kill every bit of joy in both the baby and Shea.

And he loved her too much to do that to her. He had to let her go. He thought of her warmth, her gentle caresses and the way she made him grin, and as his hand rested on the soft green velvet of her dress, he wished that she was right, that there would be a Christmas miracle. But he knew better.

Shea wished she knew what Jared was thinking. So many times during the past two days, she caught him just staring at her. She wasn't sure if he was waiting for her good spirits to cease, or for her to demand something of him, but either way, she did her best to show him nothing but love.

For the baby's sake.

The change in him had been hard to spot, but it *was* happening, ever so gradually. He played Santa with a quiet kind of spirit that captivated the kids. Then, even though he hated the suit, he'd put it back on to make Denton's annual Christmas run with her and Mack to the houses of the less well-off kids. And now he was dancing with her *not* dressed as Santa, which was the best treat of all. It almost seemed as if they could actually be happy.

Could, maybe, but she had a lingering fear. Had the change in him been deep enough to let them be happy together for real this time? And would it last?

She didn't know. All she knew was that the clock was ticking faster than she wanted it to—toward Wednesday and the divorce.

And her heart was breaking. She had to get him to stay, to realize what a wonderful man he was and that all the happiness in the world could be his if he would only start reaching out and believing in the Christmas magic that was all around him. But how?

By the time they arrived home and changed and met back downstairs, Shea had started a batch of cookies and come up with yet another project that would buy her some more time with Jared. Her father was out helping Molly and her mother pack to move over to their garage apartment, and it was a great time to get him involved in all their lives. But first, she had to convince him that he was needed.

She found him at the dining-room table, typing on his portable computer.

"I hate to interrupt you—" she started, only to be interrupted herself by the wry, half grin on Jared's face when his eyes left the computer screen and found hers.

"I'd be willing to make a little Christmas wager that you don't mind interrupting me at all," he said, pushing the computer aside. "What can I do for you, Shea?"

His eyes looked kind of sad, and an irresistible need to be closer to him drew her to his side of the oak table. "It's not for me."

"No kids tonight, Shea," he said quietly.

"You sure? It's a treat for Molly."

This time when Jared looked at her, she could tell for certain—he wasn't teasing her. His expression was closed. "I'm sure."

"Oh, okay," she said, trying her best to sound nonchalant as she left the table with a growing lump of disappointment in her throat. "No problem."

Her mom had been wrong, bless her loving heart. She'd lost. Love and laughter didn't do a thing for a person when he'd spent most of his years without any.

Walking to the door leading directly into the kitchen, she pulled the batch of cookies out of the oven. It was moments later, after they'd cooled and she'd slipped them off the rack and into the jar, that she realized she had no real desire to make any more. And as she heard Jared tapping away furiously on his laptop, she put a lid on both the cookie jar and her hopes and dreams for the baby. She leaned dejectedly against the counter, wondering if she should just go to bed.

"Oh, hell." The tapping of the computer keys stopped, and seconds later, Jared was at the kitchen door. "Okay, I give up. What does Molly need?"

She should have been elated, but instead, she felt tired, tired of fighting a battle she didn't seem to be winning. She gave him a sad smile. "I wouldn't want to force you into something you didn't want to do."

"Force?" The barest hint of a grin formed on his lips. "More like gently manipulate, I think, with those huge green eyes of yours batting at me so hopefully. You were always pretty good at getting me right where you wanted me."

"If I was that good, Jared, we would be together now."

He moved out of the doorway, found a spot next to her and leaned against the counter, his eyes twinkling. "In case you haven't noticed, we are."

Her breath caught. Whenever he got close like this, she could feel the power he had over her. The power that reminded her how much she wanted him. The good Lord help her, she would want him forever, even after their divorce went through.

"I'm going to do whatever you want me to do for Molly," he said. "The question is, why?"

She smiled at him, trapped between wanting to push him away because she was afraid to get too close, and wanting to hold him so tightly he would never go. "You're a nice guy?" she tried.

"Not that nice. What's in it for me?"

"That would depend, I think, on what you want."

"I'm thinking," he said, taking another step toward her, suddenly a whisper away.

She didn't want him to move. "You close in fast."

"Maybe it's just that the distance between us isn't as wide as we think it is." Reaching out, he brushed a lazy, swirling tendril of her dark hair away from her cheek and tucked it behind her ear, where his fingertips rested on the edge of her earlobe. They trailed down to the silver hoop she wore, one of the pair that he'd given her on her birthday. "You still have these?"

"Of course," she said simply. "They were the first present you ever gave me."

His expression quickly became a mixture of pleasure and pain. "And the last present I'm ever going to give you is our baby."

"No, Jared, that's where you're wrong," she said, shaking her head very slowly, her eyes never leaving his. "The last present you gave me was saving my

Christmas by staying long enough to frighten off the Grinch and by doing your best at playing Santa Claus for the store. I know how hard it was for you, and you have no idea how much your trying to help meant to me.''

''So tell me, how much?'' he asked, his voice thick with some unnamed emotion.

She was tempting Fate and she knew she had no right to, but she suddenly couldn't stop herself. Rising on tiptoe, she slipped both her hands around his neck and he obliged her by lowering his head until his mouth met hers. His hands came to rest on either side of her waist, and within a couple of seconds, he was pulling her toward him until her body was nestled against his.

It was a kiss that made her yearn for every single one she had missed during the months they had been apart. A deep kiss of desire that made her tighten her arms around him and want desperately to hold on to the forever he could offer.

His grip on her also tightened as he deepened the kiss, his lips pressing and probing and making her want to take him upstairs. Maybe she would have, if on the cue of her breathless sigh, the warmth of his lips against hers had not faded in intensity and he had not ended the kiss.

But he had.

Wanting to give them both some thinking room, Shea backed away, one hip against the counter to stabilize a world that had slipped off its axis. She didn't know what to say or what to do. The kiss had not assuaged the ache in her; it had just intensified her need for him. But did it really change anything?

Her eyes still caught up in the blue depths of his, she pulled in a deep breath of control. She had to say something—but what?

Jared cleared his throat. "Molly?"

"Hmm?" Whatever she'd been about to blather stuck in her throat. Shea knew she ought to be pleased he was thinking about the child; nevertheless she also couldn't help feeling a tinge of disappointment at the change in direction he'd taken.

Don't push, she reminded herself. Don't go too fast. Think about how you really feel. Don't destroy the both of you by making another mistake. But no matter how much she might tell herself that, the simple fact remained that the clock was ticking and bringing the moment of their divorce closer and closer....

While she was beginning to think she'd fallen back in love with her husband.

"Mack..." She stopped to take another deep breath and started over again. "Dad wants to string lights across the front of the garage apartment for Molly— as a surprise for when they move in. But I don't want him up on the ladder. I told him I would ask you."

"All right."

Her eyes lit up. "You'll do it?"

Jared shrugged, trying to appear nonchalant. The kiss had thrown him for a loop, and not understanding why she'd started that, he'd wanted to bolt, but the hopefulness she probably didn't even know was in her eyes had ensnared him in her Christmas spell one more time.

Put simply, he wanted to make her happier. He wanted to increase that joy. He shouldn't, because he knew he was going to have to put an end to this— tonight. He was no good for her—or their child. That was pretty evident. He didn't know how to love and never would.

He'd agreed to put up the lights not out of any great wish to make Molly's day, but rather because the waters he'd just been in with Shea had been pretty deep, to say the least. After that kiss—hell, even before that kiss—he'd been wound up like a jack-in-the-box ready to spring. Some physical exertion and cold air were exactly what he needed, along with distance from her intoxicating scent.

"Thanks," she said. Reaching up, she laid her fingers on his arm and squeezed gently, shooting bolts of desire through him. He had a suspicion she knew exactly what she was doing—getting him under her spell.

And it was working.

Damn.

On the other hand, he could be wrong. He knew they ought to have this out, that there was a whole lot more to be cleared up between them. But he couldn't do that to her. Not right now. Not after that kiss. Later, after he'd been outside in the cold and his temperature had gone back to normal, he would tell her he was leaving.

"Molly will be ecstatic," she said, still eyeing him as if she half expected him to change his mind. "I'll go call Dad and make sure he keeps Molly away until we're done.''

Jared watched her as she walked out of the room. The warmer things grew between them, the more confused he was getting. Did she want him back as he was, or was she trying to change him? And why, when she'd had plenty of chances, was she still hiding the fact that the Grinch was no longer a problem?

Having her so responsive to him, so able to ride along with even his remoteness and make him feel content again when he was with her, had definitely worn down his resistance. As he'd sat there typing, his thoughts had centered on Shea and on how much he wanted her and her warm, cozy, *perfect* life again with all his heart.

But so help him, he was still too scared. He could show her he loved her his way; he knew how to do that. But as hard as he tried, he couldn't let loose enough to feel in his heart whatever everyone else seemed to be feeling—the joy, the enthusiasm, the warmth.

And without feeling it in his heart, his relationship with Shea seemed like a poor facsimile of what he knew she wanted. That, he guessed, would end up hurting all of them if he stayed—because Shea would soon discover that he didn't want what she did with all his heart. And it would hurt her.

It occurred to him that he and Shea were total opposites—she was always inside, all heart, warm and cozy, while he was always outside, cold, braving the elements, his nose pressed up against the window, wishing for something that could never be.

Cold. That's what he needed right then and there, to be outside in the two-inch-deep snow. He headed toward the back door and was slipping on his jacket, ready to take a break from being around Shea, when he realized something.

He didn't know a damned thing about putting up Christmas lights. He was going to need her help.

It figured.

Despite the frosty air, it had been a moonlit night with shooting stars and laughter, Shea thought, her eyes watching Jared, her heart filled with peace. A night to see Santa stomping on the roof...only this Santa was wearing jeans and a parka and uttering an occasional curse.

It was a night that made her hope that the connection between her and Jared would never end. A night for wishes sent to Santa that might just come true.

"A bit more to the left with that string and it'll be centered," she told him, waving her hand in the appropriate direction.

After shifting the lights, Jared stapled them in place the way Shea had told him, connected one last plug, then climbed down the ladder. Meeting him at the bottom, she took hold of his arm and pulled, holding on perhaps a little more tightly than she needed to.

"Where are we going now?" he asked.

"To get your reward for being such a good boy," she said, shooting him a wicked, wicked grin. "I'm going to light up your night."

"Out here?" The image of her lithe body lingered before Jared's eyes, but he shook it off. "I've heard of blankets of snow, but somehow I don't think it would be as cozy as it sounds once the clothes come off.''

"That's not what I had in mind, and I think you know it." But she was smiling as she pulled him to the sidewalk at the far end of the lawn, well away from the garage. Continuing that vibrant smile and starting to hum "We Wish You a Merry Christmas," she hurried back to the garage and flipped on the outside light switch.

The darkness around the garage was lit up with red, green, blue and orange dancing twinkle lights. On the garage roof, a red-and-white outline of Santa in his sleigh sparkled merrily. Jared stared at it. He'd done that? Himself?

She was back at his side in a second. "So what do you think?"

"I think it's a child's paradise," he said gruffly, his throat thick with emotion.

"Molly's going to love it," Shea said softly. "I'll make sure she knows you did it for her."

"I didn't do it for her, Shea," he said slowly.

"Of course you did it for her." She beamed at him. "You only think you're afraid of children, Jared. Actually, you've been wonderful with them—once you warmed up, that is."

"No, I'm afraid you're wrong." He had to let her know how he felt now and why he couldn't stay, or he'd find himself unable to leave.

And he had to. He couldn't stay around to watch the baby inside her grow, watch Shea blossom into motherhood, wanting to touch her as he did but never having her again. It was best to lay it on the line, call it quits. He couldn't be this near to all her warmth, not even for one more night.

"You're still a little scared of being a father, Jared, but I've been watching you. And I know that everything will turn out fine once the baby's here."

"I don't think you should count on that," he said firmly, his gaze remaining on the lights until he couldn't stand her silence. He dropped his eyes to hers.

The glow had left her beautiful face. Jared could feel what he had of a heart breaking, but there was no helping this. He knew what he was and wasn't capable of; he knew it too damned well. It was time to let her know.

"I put up those lights because I knew they would make you happy, Shea. I went with you to get a tree you ended up hating and then out again on a wild-tree chase to get it back, then scouted out Molly's lost Santa, looked for the Grinch, played Santa Claus and went dancing with you—" he paused and took a breath "—all of it just to make you happy. None of it meant anything to me in any other way."

He knew he should walk away right then and there, not stand around and hurt her underneath the glimmer of the first Christmas lights he'd ever put up himself, but he couldn't help it. He had to make her see that it wouldn't work, that he couldn't be the perfect daddy to their beautiful baby, couldn't be a loving husband to her, because he simply didn't believe he had the warmth it took in him. He just didn't feel anything except the need to be around her. He knew there was something more that Shea was feeling. He could see it in the depths of her eyes whenever she looked at him. But he didn't have a clue how to drum it up inside himself. No matter how many Christmas activities he'd been involved in, no matter how happy he made Shea, he just couldn't feel all this *joy* that others seemed to be feeling.

He touched her cheek and wiped a crystal tear away. "All I wanted to do was make you happy, and I couldn't even be perfect at doing that. Face it, Shea. I'm never going to be the man you need, not for the baby, and not for you. I don't know how. I can go through the motions, but I can't feel it inside my heart. I almost brought you down to my level once, and I can't stick around and do it again."

Hating himself, he headed toward the house. He had to get back to his place in Topeka. It wasn't home—he would always think of home as being where Shea was, whether they were married or not. But he couldn't stick around her any longer, wishing for something that would never be.

Shea was seconds behind him as he went into the foyer. The reopening and closing of the door confirmed it.

"Please, Jared, don't go."

Slowly, he faced her, keeping more than an arm's length away. "There's no real reason for me to stay any longer, is there?" If she wouldn't let him go, then he had to make sure it was over himself. Mr. Cold Heart. He could do it. And he would hate himself every minute of the rest of his life for it, too. "No reason, because Mr. Griswold's been behaving himself quite nicely since you caught him, hasn't he?''

"You knew?"

"Let's just say I didn't waste any time before following you out of the store."

Her mouth dropped open. "You mean the Santa everyone saw waving was you? When people mentioned it to me, I couldn't believe it. I thought maybe Molly's Santa had returned. It was you?"

"Me." He nodded his head. "I was on the far side of the big tree in front of the courthouse, a few feet away from where you and Mr. Griswold had your little talk." Turning, he walked into the brightness of the kitchen and the Christmas scent of a holly berry candle, trusting she would follow.

She did—with a question.

"So you knew I found the Grinch but you didn't say anything?"

"Neither did you, sweetheart." He shot her a brief, sardonic grin as he pulled out a chair for her.

"Yeah, but me I can understand," she said, sounding more glib than she felt as she slipped off her jacket and hung it over the back of her chair. Still standing, she caught his eye again and gave him a long, searching look. "If you knew it was over, Jared, why did you stay on?"

If he didn't break Christmas spell, he was going to end up making them all miserable in the long run. "I guess I was curious," he said quietly. "When you didn't tell me about the Grinch, I wanted to see what else you were up to."

"What else? You mean you guessed what I was trying to do by making you play Santa?"

"Learn to love kids?" He stared at her incredulously. "I may not have a heart, Shea, but I do have a brain."

"Oh, Jared," she said with a long sigh, "of course you have a heart."

She sank onto her chair, looking exhausted, and Jared almost went to her. But he stiffened. He couldn't be crazy. He had to make her see why it would be best if he got out of her and the baby's lives now.

"I wanted you to stay after I found Mr. Griswold," she told him softly, gazing up at him, "to buy the time to try and make sure you had at least one merry Christmas in your life. One you would always remember."

Although he remained well away from her, Jared's expression was haunted. Perhaps he finally understood she'd been doing these things for him, even knowing they might not work. Shea supposed they hadn't if she was to believe his words. But she could have sworn he was happy during the past few days, and more than once. Like the time when he'd played Santa and been talking with the children, while he'd laughed at her jokes…and while he'd held her tightly that afternoon when they danced.

So why couldn't he see it, too?

"I guess you succeeded there," he said finally. "This *has* been one heck of a crazy Christmas. Probably," he said, "the best one I ever had."

At least she'd given him that much, Shea thought,

directly or indirectly. But it wouldn't be enough. He was still leaving. She could read it in the way he stood, in the glances he was giving her. He might be talking to her now instead of silently walking away as he used to when they'd been living together, but eventually, he was still going to walk away. Everything might have changed for him—but in reality, nothing had.

Nothing would.

"I may have shown you Christmas fun, but I haven't helped you understand the joy and the spirit that goes with it, have I?" she asked.

"It's something I guess I'll have to figure out on my own."

With his words, Shea felt the steam go out of her. She'd failed.

Uttering a soft sigh of surrender, she lifted her hand to cover a mouth that was twisting as she held back tears. "What if I tell you I like you just fine the way you are?" she asked. "And begged you to stay?"

"It won't work," Jared told her, his voice gentle. "You're everything I could have hoped for, Shea, but it won't work. Sometimes..." He gave a groan of exasperation, not knowing how to explain it to her, but realizing he had to try. "Sometimes I feel like I'll always be cold. You don't need that kind of person in your life. Neither does the baby. It needs Quiet Brook, it needs your warmth and love and...and—" he gestured widely "—and holly berry candles in the kitchen at Christmas."

Tears trickled down from her eyes. Jared's lips tightened together in a grimace as he grabbed a handful of tissues from the box on the counter and handed them to her.

"Hell, now I've made you cry." Feeling like the Grinch himself, Jared watched Shea dab at her eyes, which seemed huge to him. Wide and beautiful. It was killing him not to reach over and pull her into his arms.

"I'm sorry," she said. "But can't you see? You're choosing to bury yourself."

"Hell," he said, sounding even more exasperated than before. "I'm not *choosing* to be this way. I *am* this way. There's a difference."

She shook her head. "No, you're choosing it. And as long as you think you can't feel love, as long as you don't open up your heart and risk the hurt, you aren't going to feel it."

Jared waited quietly for her to get it all out. She deserved the chance to give him what-for. She'd tried harder than anyone else ever had to make him happy.

"You're still leaving, aren't you?" she asked, her voice a whisper.

He nodded solemnly.

"You're going to end up alone and crotchety like your father," she warned, wiping away more tears.

"I know," he admitted. "But you see, Shea, I can't even feel anything about that. It's as if it was destined. I think it would be easier if we just said our goodbyes and started learning how to become polite strangers."

She took a deep breath, feeling like he'd just shattered her heart into a million pieces of ice. "Don't go, Jared. I love you any way you are."

His dark blue eyes seared into her. "This is already too damned hard for me, Shea. Please don't make it worse."

"Fine." He was frozen solid again, she could see it in the way he held himself and in the shuttered look in his eyes. But all she could do was love him. "You do what you need to. But know that I love you—I always will. If you start believing in that kind of magic again, Jared, you know where I'll be."

With a last, long look at her, Jared reached over and brushed a tear away from her cheek. "I'm sorry, sweetheart."

She couldn't reply. A few seconds later, she didn't have to because he'd left her alone in the kitchen. Shea lowered her cheek down to her folded arms on the tabletop. It was over. She'd given her best as well as her heart, and she didn't know how else to reach him anymore.

But she knew better, didn't she? Nothing could save her marriage now, not even Santa Claus—and she used to believe *he* could do anything. Jared had once said he wished she would understand that sometimes life couldn't be as perfect as she wanted it. He'd been right. Saving her marriage was going to take a Christmas miracle.

The problem was, though, just like Jared, she wasn't sure she believed in them any longer.

Chapter Ten

The hell of it was, while Jared couldn't muster out of the emptiness inside him any feelings he imagined were profound joy and love, back in Topeka, on his own again, he quickly discovered that he sure could plumb the depths of misery and anger. Just thinking he would no longer have any real claims to Shea made him want to bash in walls. So much so that when his lawyer told him on Monday that he didn't have to be in the courtroom late Wednesday when the judge issued the decree, Jared told him to go ahead without him and not to call him afterward—just mail him his decree and his bill.

After that, trying to pretend Shea and his baby didn't exist, Jared worked in his office. Then on a stakeout far into the night. Home briefly for a quick shower and a change of clothes. Back in his office. All day. Into the night. Working hard so he didn't have to think about how much he didn't want to be on the outside looking in anymore, and how that would never happen. He wanted to feel numb, but that was a feeling only exhaustion seemed to bring. So he worked some more.

He'd been working so hard, in fact, that on the evening his divorce supposedly became final without him, when the grandfather clock in the corner of his office—a gift from Shea he'd never had the heart to get rid of—bonged ten times, he thought he heard a deep voice calling his name. Jared jerked awake with a start, having fallen asleep at his desk.

"Well, finally!" the voice boomed again. "I thought I was going to have to call out a rescue squad!"

Jared blinked quickly, his wits waking up faster than his weary body, and finally, slowly, his eyes focused in on the speaker, an old man with a white beard and a red-and-white velvet suit and hat, standing on the other side of his desk. He looked strangely like...Santa Claus.

Not that there was such a thing.

"It's way too quiet in here." Walking over to a radio on Jared's bookcase, Santa picked out a station with Christmas music and left it playing softly in the background. "There, that's better."

Watching the guy, Jared realized he hadn't locked his office door before he'd passed out from exhaustion. Brilliant. Leaning forward, ready to react if necessary, he placed his right hand over the edge of the drawer where he kept his gun and regarded the man warily. With the great cynicism of those who have been there and seen everything lacing his voice, Jared said, "*Santa,* right?"

"Good, good, we have that cleared up right away," the visitor said, his deep voice rumbling merrily. "I haven't got all day, you know!" he added. "There's plenty for me to do back home, packing up toys for the children. It isn't easy." He wagged one of his white-gloved fingers at Jared. "But do you care? Nooo! Sleeping the evening away, when you could be out there doing something useful."

"This is not a good dream," Jared said to himself. "But that would be silly, because who would have nightmares about Santa?"

Santa grinned, held on to his belly and laughed. "Exactly, my boy, exactly!"

It had to be a dream, Jared told himself, but even so, he began to slide the desk drawer open with his fingertips just in case Santa's irritation with him turned into something worse.

"A gun?" Santa threw back his head and laughed again. "Ho, ho, ho, boy, you won't need that. Here, let me show you I'm harmless." Reaching inside a massive pocket Jared remembered only too well, Santa pulled out candy canes, lollipops, a couple of small cars and a Santa on a rocking chair and piled them all on Jared's desk. Finished, the bearded man tapped on the Santa toy and set it to rocking. "I'm kind of fond of that one myself," he said, grinning at Jared.

When Jared didn't grin back, Santa then turned his other pocket inside out, sat down and slipped out of his boots, presenting each foot for Jared's perusal. His socks had little Christmas trees on them. Once his boots were back on, he stood and stomped his feet. "Is that good enough, son? I hope so, because we need to get down to business."

Jared still felt wary. "You need to hire me?"

"Well, not me exactly. This concerns a little friend of mine I met in Quiet Brook. Molly." All merriment disappeared from Santa's sky blue eyes as he reloaded the small toys into his pockets. "You're needed in Quiet Brook, son. You have to go back there—now. I'd go myself, but I can't help everybody—there aren't enough hours in a day."

Jared got the drift that this must be Molly's transient Santa. The question was, what the hell was he doing here in Topeka? And in *his* office? And since "Santa" was here, how would the man know what was going on sixty miles away? Jared wanted to tell him to hit the road, but the same feeling he'd once had that Molly had turned up in his life for a reason came rushing back full force, and he couldn't.

"What about Molly?" he asked.

"Sad situation." Santa shook his head, his eyes worried as they peered down at Jared over his wire-rimmed glasses. "I kept telling her I couldn't give her this particular Christmas wish, but I'm afraid she didn't listen. She keeps believing in me, and, well, it's going to lead to disaster for her, and maybe for your wife if she goes outside in this weather, and with her big heart, I know she might. But I really can't do a thing myself—you need to go back to Quiet Brook."

A feeling of dread had slowly built up inside Jared

as the man added word after word to his scenario. "What do you mean 'disaster'?" he asked quickly, wondering if he should call in the police.

"For Molly." Santa reached up under his hat and felt around, then pulled out a folded piece of paper, which he opened and read. "'Dear Santa.'" He paused and looked at Jared. "That's me." At Jared's scowl he cleared his throat and continued. "'I have an important Christmas wish to tell you. Please come to the park tonight. I'll be there.'" Rattling the paper in his hand, Santa peered over his glasses again directly at Jared. "There's more, but I gave you the important stuff. I took it out of Denton's Santa mailbox when I was passing through earlier, but I didn't get to read it until just a little while ago. That's why I'm so late. You've got to hurry."

As he said that, the clock chimed the quarter hour, and Santa's eyes widened. "Oh, no. Got to catch the 10:20 back to the Pole. The missus needs me. Says things are gettin' a little behind." He wiggled his eyebrows and put the paper in his pocket.

Jared shook his head as he watched Santa hurrying toward the door. He had to be dreaming.

Santa stopped, gave him a last look, then shook his head in disgust. "You're dawdling! There's no time to waste. If you leave right away, you might just stop a catastrophe and get everything you ever wanted for Christmas."

"That's impossible," Jared replied, looking up— but the door was just swinging shut, and the man was already gone.

Scowling, he hurried to the door, pushed it open

and looked outside through the falling snow in time to see the tail end of a red suit disappearing around the corner. He started to chase him down toward the end of the strip mall, but then the wind starting whipping up and blew a piece of paper right onto his pants leg, distracting him. When he kicked it away, he happened to notice it had the same odd green Christmas tree with the same multicolored gifts that Molly had shown him when he'd been playing Santa.

Scowling, he returned to the office so he could decipher the words in the light. He could read "park" and "come" and "Santa," but it didn't look like a child had written them. However, there was no mistaking that tree and the word "Molly" beside it.

"Hell." Did he believe all this, or not? Every logical bone in his body told him just to call Shea and ask her to check on the kid since Molly was now living right across the yard from her. He knew she wouldn't be particularly thrilled to hear from him, but this was too strange to ignore.

So he tapped out Shea's number. Busy.

Scowling, he got the number for the sheriff's office, but he got repeated busy signals there, too, for over ten minutes. The operator told him the line might be down because of the storm. In Quiet Brook, that happened, and the weather didn't even have to be that bad.

Jared rose and went for his jacket. He knew the guy couldn't be Santa Claus—Molly was just a kid whose bright, hopeful eyes were filled with a trust in Christmas magic. He didn't know what her wish was, but he thought it had to be really important for her to venture out in the dark for it.

But making sure she got her wish, whatever it was, was not why he was yanking on his jacket, shutting off the lights and locking the door to his office. He swore it wasn't. If he was going to give anyone her wish, it would be Shea.

No, he was hopping into his truck for the sole reason that if Molly went to the park at night because she thought Santa would be coming, that wasn't good. Anything could happen.

Anything. Because as much as Shea wanted her little corner of the world to be perfect, it wasn't. A stranger had Molly's letter to Santa. A stranger knew Molly was going to the park. A total stranger had mentioned Shea's name particularly in the same breath as catastrophe.

Shoving the gearshift into reverse, he backed out of his parking spot. He didn't want to set foot near Shea, didn't want to feel that pain again, but a wildly cascading tension in his gut warned him to check out this Santa's story. Every ounce of his common sense was telling him to get to Quiet Brook.

And to hurry.

As the wind gusted snow into her face, Shea tucked her muffler higher up around her cheeks, waved her flashlight into the darkness of the park and called Molly's name again.

No answer.

She shouldn't be out in this weather, she knew, not with visibility poor and every step under her holding

icy potential for a fall. But she'd felt guilty staying
inside with most of the town out searching for the
little girl who had turned up missing. So when she'd
remembered that Molly had asked her to spell out
"park" and a couple of other words on a letter to
Santa a couple of days before, then found the phones
were dead so she couldn't report it to anyone, she'd
known what she needed to do.

Besides, she couldn't stand being alone with her
misery for one minute longer. She wanted Jared so
badly she was getting no joy out of the holiday, no
peace from the Christmas hymns. All she could think
about was how terribly wrong she'd been to try to
change him when she should have loved him just the
way he was and made him understand that. No wonder he'd thought he would make her miserable if he
stayed. By trying to change him, she had given him
the impression that he wasn't fine just the way he was.

She'd always been like that, wanting everything
fixed to her own satisfaction. Well, she'd learned.
She'd really learned that some things are best just as
they are.

Like the love you already had.

"Molly!" she shouted again, and the wind carried
the word in an eerie spiral of snow away from her.
She was scared for the little girl, frightened that she
could slip and hurt her and Jared's child, and more
than that even, morose over how stupid she'd been
about Jared.

A couple of tears fell and froze on her muffler. She
shook her head. She couldn't cry. She had to get
tough and cope, just the way Jared had done his

whole life. If Molly was indeed out here, and she remained tough, she could stick it out and find the child. If she started crying, she might as well go sit in the car and give up.

On everything.

And she didn't want to do that. She wanted to take what she had and make a joyous season out of it that lasted a lifetime. And what she had was Jared. She needed to fight for him, show him she valued him above everything. Convince him that she and their baby were going to be fine with the one man who loved them in his own way more than anything else in the world.

"Molly!" she called more loudly, feeling a renewed strength. She was going to look just a few more minutes for the little girl, then she was going to trust that the child wasn't there. After that she was going to drive to Topeka and beg Jared to take her back no matter what she had to do.

Carefully treading past the swing set, Shea heard what she thought was a faint cry for help but might only have been a gust of icy wind. She called Molly's name once more but heard nothing in response.

Her imagination. She wanted the child to be found so much she was hearing her voice. Blinking fiercely against the snow, she walked a few more steps past the seesaws to check the gully on the far side of the park. Just in case.

And that's when she heard the voice again—one tiny cry for help, and then another one.

Having spent a lot of afternoons in that park in her childhood, ingrained instinct told Shea to stop at the point where she otherwise might have fallen down the six-foot slide into the gully, which was in reality a wide drainage ditch walled by dirt.

She swiftly unwrapped her muffler and called, "Honey, it's Shea! Where are you?"

"Down here," Molly cried weakly. "I hurt my foot." She let out a whimper, then added, "When I fell."

In the circle of light from her flashlight, Shea spotted the girl halfway down the side. "Sweetie, the whole town has been looking for you. I have to go call your mama, then I'll come down there and sit with you." She hoped the phones were working again. If they weren't, she would have to go down the block to get to the nearest house.

"No! Please don't leave. I'm scared," Molly said, starting to cry. "I'm cold."

"Honey, it's going to be all right," Shea reassured her, although she wasn't too certain about that herself. "I'll come down and give you the flashlight and then I'll go the car. It's not going to take very long, I promise."

Sitting very carefully, refusing to worry about the possibility of falling herself, Shea dug her heels into the snow and made her way down a half-dozen feet of hill. When she got to Molly, the little girl promptly snuggled up against her and wrapped her arms around her waist.

"Don't leave. Please don't leave. Santa's coming. You've got to be here."

Shea gently pried the child away from her, took the muffler from around her own neck and wrapped the little girl's head with it. They were partially protected from the wind in the gully, but somehow the snow seemed heavier there. And Molly was shivering badly.

"Santa? How do you know?"

"I wrote him a letter and put it in the special place under the Santa Box where Santa told me to leave it when he was here. When I checked later, it was gone, I told him to come to the park so I could tell him my Christmas wish 'cause Mommy said I couldn't see him anymore 'cause he left town."

"Why didn't you just write him the wish in the letter?"

Molly shook her head and buried her face against Shea. "I wanted to talk to him. 'Cause he left without saying goodbye, and I wanted to make sure he wasn't mad at me or nothing." Her voice, already quiet, had grown softer and softer as she snuggled against Shea. "But I'm all right, 'cause you're here now, and Santa's coming."

That wasn't the way it was, Shea wanted to tell the child. They could get frostbitten or some other horrible thing if they remained down in the gully much longer, assuming Molly wasn't already, and at the worst... She didn't even want to think of that.

She dared not.

Huddled there with Molly, she tried to drum up some Christmas spirit, but she couldn't.

She had none left.

Cursing, sure he'd seen the damned park somewhere on the street near the church where their imperfect tree had ended up, Jared cut his engine in front of the church, got out and walked back toward the corner, letting the cold air give him strength. Crossing, he continued to walk past the houses with Christmas lights aglow through the windows, his fear for Molly and Shea growing with every step.

He'd made good time, but it was after eleven at night. Shea should have been home. But not even Lucy Millstone's old sedan had been parked in the Dentons' driveway. In fact, the Dentons' garage door had been left open, making him figure that Shea had gone somewhere in a hurry.

And that scared him to death.

Stop a catastrophe, Molly's Santa had said. How would the old man know what was going on—unless...?

No, he told himself sternly. That Santa Claus actually existed was just too crazy a notion to consider. Trudging through the snow, he sank knee-deep into drifts, but he kept going farther, down the opposite side of the long street where he hadn't driven earlier. He wasn't going to stop. Not till he found her. Shea.

A fierce longing catapulted through him. He had to get Shea back. His world wouldn't be right without her in it. She was like the missing piece of the puzzle that was him. He didn't even know what he was thinking anymore—he just knew that every inch of him wanted her safe in his arms. The feeling had been growing in intensity all during the ride to Quiet Brook, and now his need for her had become too painful to ignore.

He glided over a small icy patch onto a street and

climbed back up another curb, then forward a few more feet...and that's when he saw it. Shea's car. And to his left was a half acre of cleared land nestled between the corner on one side and woods on the other. The park.

Scanning the area with his flashlight, he saw nothing except the swings and seesaws and some climbing contraption. The park went farther back than he'd thought, the distance of a whole block, maybe more. Near the trees, he squinted, thinking he saw the land dipping a little, but he wasn't sure.

That was when he saw the stream of gentle light that seemed to point right to a spot on the earth, illuminating the now-dancing snowflakes. The light wavered briefly, then went out. It took him a few breathless seconds before he realized the light hadn't come from heaven downward, but rather from someone's flashlight, upward. Shea's flashlight. It had to be.

His heart in his throat, he hurried toward the spot where he'd seen the light, praying for the first time since he'd been a child. He'd never felt a longing as intense as this one, never in his whole life.

Love.

It had to be.

If it wasn't, it was the closest he thought he would ever come. He was truly feeling it again—at least he thought so. The intensity of it drove him forward, toward the gully, toward his other half.

The wind died down as he neared the spot, and the snowflakes let up until they disappeared altogether.

He could hear Shea talking. Her soft voice drew him like a magnet, his heart pounding.

"Can you move your foot at all?" Shea asked. A couple seconds later, Jared heard a tiny gasp. "Okay, then I *have* to climb back up and call for help. Molly, sweetheart, I have no choice."

"Don't want you to. Santa will come."

They both sounded like they would make it to morning, and Jared breathed a sigh of relief. As he approached the incline, he slowed down so he wouldn't slip himself and heard Shea say, "Molly, I can't argue with you now. Santa probably didn't get your letter and he probably won't come. You have to remember that life isn't a fairy tale."

"No, she doesn't," Jared called over the side so they both could hear, but he was speaking mainly to Shea. "And neither do you." With his flashlight pointed near them, he could see Shea's eyes widen in pure shock. "Smile, ladies," he said, grinning at Shea. "'Cause Santa is here."

A frighteningly pale Molly smiled weakly up at him, then turned her trusting gaze back on Shea. "See, told ya he'd come."

Crunching through ice, Jared half stepped, half skidded down the slope. Once he was braced against falling, he handed his flashlight to Shea, stripped off his jacket and wrapped it around Molly. He didn't even feel the cold, not with the warmth and love shining on him from Shea's eyes.

"Who's hurt?" he asked.

"Molly's ankle, I think," Shea told him.

He reached over and cupped Shea's cheek tenderly, surrounding it with his warmth. "How about you?"

"I'll be all right," she whispered. "Now that you're back."

He grinned. "That's what I wanted to hear."

She hesitated. "But how did you know where we were?"

Jared knew that Molly should be taken to the doctor's without delay. But something inside him told him that any kind of hurry might alarm the child, so he grinned down at Molly and was relieved when she smiled back up at him. In perfect unison, they said the answer together. "Santa."

Molly giggled weakly. "I was going to ask Santa to send Jared back here to town 'cause I missed him, and you missed him, and he makes a funny Santa Claus."

"I make a funny Santa." Jared hoisted Molly into his arms. "Gee, is this the thanks I get for saving you?"

Giggling again, Molly nestled against him, just as she had against Shea. "Only how did Santa know what my wish was?"

"Oh, I'd say Santa knows what's in everyone's heart," Jared told her earnestly. "In fact, he told me if I came and saved you, I would get everything I ever wanted for Christmas."

"Will you?"

"That depends," he said, looking down as Shea started to get up. "I guess we'll have to see."

Rising carefully, Shea moved the light so she could

see his face. "I think Jared will get every single thing he wants for Christmas. All he'll have to do is ask."

Molly had a sprained ankle, but, just as she had sworn to Jared, Shea suffered no ill effects from exposure. Two hours after Jared had rescued them from the snowy slope, she was snuggled in Jared's arms on the couch downstairs in her father's home, fully clothed and smiling about Mack's stern warning that they couldn't share a bed until they were married again. Jared had filled her in about his visit from Santa, but she still could hardly believe it.

She went up on her elbow to gaze at him. A soft light from one corner of the room lit his dark features. She'd never loved him more than she had the second he'd shown up on that hillside because he'd been worried about the fate of a child.

Her holiday hero.

"Do you think it was Molly's homeless Santa from the Shelter?"

"You never know," he said, sounding like he might.

Propped up on the pillows, Jared grinned at her. "Does it matter who he was?"

"I guess it is more fun to just *believe.*" And it made her happy, too. "He brought you back to me, which is all that matters anyway. But I'm surprised you didn't just call and send someone to the park."

"I tried. Phones were out." He ran his finger down the lock of her hair to where it lay on her shoulder. "That guy—Santa—said you might be headed for a catastrophe. I knew I had to come."

His fingertips drew swirls on the top of her collar-bone, sending heat into the far reaches of her body. Reaching up, she drew his head down and kissed him, melting back into the pillows. His hand caressed her rib cage and came to rest on top of their growing child.

"I want to stay, Shea," he said, his voice husky with emotion. "I realized on the way over that I was never going to make it without you. That something deep inside me longed for you so badly I couldn't stand it. That if I was ever going to know love, it was going to be because of you."

"That already sounds like love," Shea told him, her fingers stroking through the hair at his temple. "It really truly does."

"It took being scared out of my mind to feel it again."

"Again?"

"Last time I remember feeling that way, it was when my aunt died and it seemed like I was all alone in the world. I don't think I let myself feel anything again after that." He cupped the side of her head. "I certainly don't want our baby to ever go through something like that. At least if we're together, maybe we can convince him his dad loves him the best way he knows how."

"Oh, Jared," she whispered. "You do want our baby?"

He nodded solemnly. "Playing Santa showed me kids aren't as scary as I thought. I mean, it's not that hard to keep them happy."

"They just want love, like anyone else." She

stroked the side of his face, delighting in the feel of his growing whiskers. "Besides, they come in handy. If the kids hadn't needed a Santa, Dad would never have sent for you, and Molly wouldn't have met you and written to Santa and we might never have gotten together again."

"You have a point." His hand inched down and crept under the bottom of her sweater. "Are you sure I have to sleep down here? I don't want to let you out of my arms."

She gave him a wide grin. "Mack's been like a father to you. Are you sure you want to break his house rules?"

He pressed against her hip. "What do you think?"

Tensing her muscles against him, she grinned back. "I think it's time to give you your Christmas present."

He groaned as she pushed herself off the couch. Then, looking resigned, he maneuvered until he was lying flat on his back against the bed pillows Shea had brought for him and waited for her. Disappearing around the corner, she was back in a flash with a present wrapped in blue-and-silver paper and topped by a matching bow. Smiling from ear to ear, she put it on his chest.

"That's your, what, fourth present to me?" Jared said. "But I haven't gotten you anything—yet."

"You gave me our baby, remember?" Sitting on the floor next to him, she leaned over and kissed him again. As he cupped her head and moved sideways, his present slid onto the floor next to her. Laughing, she picked it up and handed it to him. "Open it."

"I still say we should wait for Christmas morning."

"Trust me, Jared," she said, about to burst with anticipation. "You want to open this *now*."

So he did, tearing off the wrapping paper and lifting the lid from the box. Inside were torn pieces of a paper that looked like it might have once been a document. Confused, he picked one up and read it, then picked up two more, read them and quickly put together what she had given him—figuratively, that was. He didn't really want to literally put the pieces back together. They were the divorce papers.

"You didn't go through with it?"

She shook her head. "I went to the courthouse dreading the whole idea, and when you didn't show up, something told me to back out. Your lawyer said something about mailing you a letter because you'd told him not to call." She took the box, placed it on the floor and gave it a little shove out of the way, then leaned over him. Her heart was filled with a love for him unlike anything she'd ever felt before. "We're still married, Jared—in the eyes of the law and one very strict father with house rules left over from the fifties. So what do you think?"

He gave her a very wide grin. "I think that you give the very best Christmas gifts in the whole world." He stood up, then lifted her up into his arms in one fell swoop. "Now let's see what Santa can conjure up for you, okay?"

She wrapped her arms around his neck. "I think that would be…a fairy-tale ending to this Christmas story, don't you?"

His remark was lost in their kiss.

Epilogue

Exactly one year later

"Erin says Santa Claus is downstairs and she wants to go see him with both of us."

Shea looked up at the doorway to her office at Denton's to see Jared standing there, his serious, dark blue eyes intent on her, with their six-month-old daughter resting against his shoulder.

"And how would you know that?" Shea let out a peal of light laughter, and Erin's eyes flitted toward her.

"I dunno," Jared said. "Last Christmas, when I played Santa, the kids must have taught me." He closed the distance between them and handed Erin to Shea. "I didn't even realize it until Erin was about a month old and I started understanding every word she said."

Shea grinned. "And why am I finding this out only now?"

"What?" Jared asked, trying to look totally serious. "She didn't tell you?"

She laughed again, tickled by the way Jared was teasing her, and nuzzled her cheek against Erin's. "Okay, baby girl. Let's go downstairs and see Santa." She moved out from behind her desk and walked toward the door. "Thanks for walking her around so I could finish up, Jared. I know you must be as tired as I am."

"Wouldn't have missed a chance to chat with my baby before she snoozes," Jared said, picking up Erin's diaper bag and turning off the office light.

Holding her baby close, Shea gazed at her husband. Jared had found a suite in an office building near the mall so he'd be closer to Quiet Brook, where they now lived in an older rambling home near the park. Shea had returned to the store in October, with Erin staying half a day with her at the office and half a day with her new grandma, Lucy Millstone, who had married Mack and now was a stay-at-home mom. Shea couldn't have been happier about the marriage. Not just because of her father, but because it meant that she'd have Molly for a sister while Erin would have a grandmother and an aunt—a family. A whole family, with a wonderful dad who loved her enough to hear what she said when she didn't say a word.

Jared stayed close behind her the whole way down, and she thanked her stars for the Christmas miracle that had come to Quiet Brook one year ago that night on a snowy bank.

As they approached the Santa Station, Shea saw Santa stashing his hat under the chair as he sat there, alone, waiting. Someone had put the Santa and Elf on Break sign out, which would explain the lack of children in line even though the store was bustling. Telling herself to remember to flip the sign after the baby visited with Santa, Shea walked up the ramp with her daughter, Jared right behind.

"Well, at last!" Santa exclaimed. "I was beginning to think you two were never coming!" He looked from Shea to the baby and then at Jared. "Told you you'd get exactly what you wanted, didn't I?"

Shea glanced over her shoulder at Jared. He was staring down at Santa as though he'd seen a ghost.

"What's going on?" she asked.

"Shea, that's him," Jared told her. "From last Christmas. Santa."

"Really?" Shea asked, handing Erin to Santa. "Molly's Santa?"

"The one and only," Santa said, laughing.

"Where's the store Santa we hired?"

"Must still be on break." The big, jolly man gave Erin a cuddle and cooed softly to her, and she in turn gurgled and smiled. Then, standing, Santa handed the baby back to Shea. "Good. Now that I'm positive you two will be fine, I've got to be going. Lots of people to check on. Busy year."

Santa hustled down the ramp, leaving Shea feeling as if she'd been hit by a whirlwind. "Uh, Santa, wait a minute."

The man stopped and looked over his shoulder as

Jared slipped an arm around Shea's waist and squeezed her gently.

"What did Erin ask you to bring her for Christmas?"

Santa's booming "Ho, ho, ho," seemed to fill the store, stopping shoppers in their tracks. "How do I know? It's Jared who can talk to her. I'm just like you—I have to wait until she's old enough to say people words." Laughing, he disappeared from sight.

Now what was she supposed to make of that? Shaking her head and chuckling, Shea turned to Jared and handed their daughter to him. "You heard him, you former Santa you. What does your daughter want for Christmas?"

Jared leaned close until his ear was near Erin's delicate mouth and, for a few seconds, nodded sagely at her every coo. At last, just when Shea thought she could wait no longer, he looked at her and smiled. "Erin says a baby brother, when her mama feels ready."

Delight spreading through her, Shea took her daughter back in her arms. She had to ask even though she knew the answer. In her heart, she knew. "So, Erin, is that your daddy talking, or you?" Baby Erin gurgled. Lifting her eyes, Shea settled her gaze on her husband, who was grinning. "Okay, wise guy, translate."

Somehow Jared kept a straight face, but his eyes twinkled with that same look her father got every year around Christmas. "Why would you even ask?"

"And how do you suppose I get this baby brother someone here wants?" she asked.

Sitting down in the Santa chair, Jared reached under it and pulled out the cap Santa had forgotten to take with him. Pulling it on his head, he grinned up at her.

"All you have to do is ask Santa."

* * * * *

Take 2 bestselling love stories FREE

Plus get a FREE surprise gift!

COMING NEXT MONTH

#1342 THE BOSS AND THE BEAUTY —Donna Clayton
Loving the Boss

Cindy Cooper dreamed of marrying her boss, even though she doubted handsome executive Kyle Prentice would look twice at a plain Jane like her. But when Cindy's true beauty was revealed, could she trust that Kyle's sudden attraction was more than skin-deep?

#1343 A RUGGED RANCHIN' DAD—Kia Cochrane
Fabulous Fathers

Stone Tyler loved his wife and his son, but tragedy had divided his family. Now this rugged rancher would do everything in his power to be the perfect daddy—and recapture his wife's heart—before time ran out....

#1344 MARRY ME, KATE—Judy Christenberry
The Lucky Charm Sisters

He needed to prevent his mother from pushing him up the aisle. She needed money to rebuild her father's dream. So William Hardison and Kate O'Connor struck a bargain. They'd marry for one year, and their problems would be solved. It was the perfect marriage—until a little thing called love complicated the deal....

#1345 GRANTED: A FAMILY FOR BABY—Carol Grace
Best-Kept Wishes

All Suzy Fenton wanted was a daddy for her sweet son. But sexy sheriff Brady Wilson thought his able secretary was looking for Mr. Right in all the wrong places. And that maybe, just maybe, her future husband was right before her eyes....

#1346 THE MILLION-DOLLAR COWBOY—Martha Shields
Cowboys to the Rescue

She didn't like cowboys, but rodeo champion Travis Eden made Becca Lawson's pulse race. Maybe it was because they had grown up together or because Travis was unlike any cowboy she had ever met. Or maybe it was purely a matter of the heart....

#1347 FAMILY BY THE BUNCH—Amy Frazier
Family Matters

There was never any doubt that rancher Hank Whittaker wanted a family—he just wasn't expecting five children all at once! Or beautiful Nessa Little, who came with them. Could Nessa convince the lone cowboy to take this ready-made family into his heart?